Life by Pumpkin

Book 2

A Cat's Tale

Life by Pumpkin

Book 2

A Cat's Tale

Leslie Popp

First paperback edition April 2024

Book design by Leslie Popp

ISBN: 979-8-9881025-3-3

In loving memory of Pumpkin, who brought so much love and joy into my life and to all those around him. Thinking of the many sweet moments resulting from his unflagging curiosity always warms my heart. The following stories recount actual events from Pumpkin's point of view. I hope they make you smile.

- Leslie

Table of Contents

Introduction by Pumpkin

W elcome loyal readers! I have become quite famous after publishing my first book, *Life by Pumpkin: A Cat's View on Everything*, in which I share my honest opinions and provide a rare window into my daily life. I assume that you absolutely adored me in that tale and have now returned for more coveted insight and life advice.

If you are confused right now and realize that you have not read my first book, then I must insist that you immediately track down my original work and spend the rest of your day catching up on my many adventures. I'll take a nap while you do that, so just wake me up when you're ready to resume.

....

Now that you're up to speed and have familiarized yourself with my writing, I have to ask—am I not the most adorable tabby cat ever?

That's a rhetorical question because, obviously, the answer is yes. With my dashing good looks, elegant stripes, and perfectly pointed ears, who wouldn't think I'm handsome?

Anyway, getting back to the reason that you're here, I'm sure you're anxious for me to impart my valuable knowledge, and in a moment, I shall do just that. Since writing my last book, I have spent time considering what topics would be most useful for training you to obey and interact with your cat. I assume you have a cat since you're reading this book about a brilliant cat and his philosophical teachings. If you don't have a cat, you should hurry to your local animal shelter and rescue one in order to fully utilize the knowledge that I'm about to share. I'll wait while you do that.

....

Now that you have a cat and have read my original book, the following lessons will make more sense. If you are wondering how a cat can write a book, you are not alone. This is a very common question, and I imagine the process is similar to how you would approach this daunting task. Usually, I sit atop, half-on, or beside Mom's folding device with the black squares and the bright screen, which I have recently learned is called a laptop. I think deep thoughts and let them seep into the device, translating them into the pages that you are now reading. During this process, I often drift off into a peaceful slumber and dream up my next captivating chapter. During the editing phase, I sit on Mom's lap while she balances the device on one leg and instruct her to make changes and rewrite passages until I'm satisfied with the final product. This can be a tiresome process, but I've got time to spare.

When we're ready for the cover art, I am transported in style to a lovely estate where paparazzi take photos of me all afternoon. The background and lighting must be perfect to highlight my silky fur and elegant whiskers. I then scrutinize the photo options, select my favorite, change my mind four times, and at last, we have a winner.

When the first copy of the book is delivered and presented to me for inspection, I lie on top of it for a while, second-guessing whether I truly want to share my teachings with the world. Eventually, I decide that the contents are far too important to be kept secret, and I would be doing society a disservice by not sharing my thoughts far and wide. At this point, I sniff the finished product, scrutinize the printing for any defects, push it off the table to test its aerodynamic properties, and wander away to let Mom handle the rest. I'll settle for nothing less than perfection.

Knowing all of the hard work that went into the production of this book, I hope you will give it the time and attention it deserves, apply the many lessons when spoiling your cat, and tell all of your friends about me. I appreciate all of my adoring fans; however, my number one fan will always be my mom. She loves me unconditionally and has given me the perfect forever home.

Forever Home

My story begins many years ago when I was serving time behind bars. They never told me what crime I had committed, but I felt sure that it couldn't have been anything too severe. Perhaps I had taken a bit of extra food, spilled my water dish on occasion, and woken my humans in the dead of night a few too many times, but those minor infractions couldn't possibly merit this prolonged confinement.

I spent a year in that cell, watching my neighbors in their compartments and observing the humans that delivered food, water, and a bit of attention on a daily basis. I would often press my face against the metal bars and daydream about running free and jumping onto a nearby shelf to get the lay of the land. I imagined sprinting back and forth between the aisles of metal boxes and hoped that one day I could make that dream come true.

Given there was little to do and nowhere to go, I became familiar with the ins and outs of the operations and grew well acquainted with the residents of the adjacent cages. There was a noisy neighbor above me that meowed periodically and grew more insistent when a person approached his cage. I never saw him, but I would know that meow anywhere. Sometimes we exchanged a few words, but there wasn't much to talk about, and we mainly discussed our food and toys. There was a skittish cat across the aisle who tended to shy away from people when her cage was opened and fresh food was offered. I encouraged her to interact with the humans because that was the best part of the day. If she was friendly and cute, they would surely pet her, which would be beneficial for her well-being. With my encouragement and the support of others in nearby cages, she began to relax and learned how to entice humans into a back scratch or a head pat.

At night, the humans would go home and leave us to our own devices. If only we could crack the complex locking system on the doors, we could party all night long and leap from one metal box to the next. We talked about this often and always hoped that one of our cages would accidentally be left open, but that never happened.

The only method of escape centered on selecting a friendly-looking human and convincing them to rescue you. I wasn't sure where my cellmates went once they were paired with a family, but there were whispers of wonderful forever homes with loving people. Those rumors gave us hope, and I was determined to keep my spirits up. Day in and day out, I would do my best to look cute and welcoming so a nice person would help me bust out of this place, but the days dragged on, and it became more difficult to muster the energy.

Then one day, a small woman knelt in front of my door and peered in. She had big brown eyes and a kind face, and she spoke in a soothing tone. My ears perked up, and I felt my heart skip a beat. She flipped the lock, swung open the bars, and perched at the entrance to my cell.

I rose to my feet, trying to seem happy and energetic even though I felt nervous and slightly stiff from lying in one place for too long. She extended her hand, and I sniffed it cautiously. She didn't rush me, and after a few moments, I cautiously rubbed my head against her arm. I was rewarded with a back rub and a soothing head scratch. I inched closer, purring softly. The rhythmic motion was calming, and my anxiety began to abate.

I glanced up and realized that she was beaming at me with an expression of pure joy. Emotions welled up within me, and I appreciated every second of her affection and undivided attention. She spoke tenderly and stroked the itchy spot on my cheek. I closed my eyes and heaved a loud sigh.

She scooted closer, and I leaned against her and peered out at the long aisle. I could have sprung forward and made a run for it, but a part of me wanted to remain by her side. I was conflicted, but I decided to stay put and wait for her next move.

I grew bolder as the minutes passed and hesitantly extended one paw onto her lap and then the other. When she didn't protest, I climbed onto her legs, and she wrapped her arms around me protectively. Then she bent forward, and I pressed my forehead to hers. We held perfectly still for a blissful moment, and the world came to a halt. All I could hear was her soft breathing and my rumbling purr. I sniffed her nose, her cheeks, and her hair before rubbing my face against her. I wanted to claim her for myself and let the other cats know that she was taken. We sat like this for a long while, and I eventually drifted off to sleep, listening to the rhythm of her heartbeat.

When I awoke, another woman was speaking to the nice lady in my cage, and I watched them groggily for a few minutes. This new woman glanced at the sign hanging on my cell door before calling me, "Pumpkin." The lady holding me smiled and repeated it, and my name had never sounded so sweet. I snuggled closer to her, sighing contentedly.

Life by Pumpkin: A Cat's Tale

The visit ended far too soon, and after she left, I watched for her every day. While the days were long, I held on to that beautiful memory, and to my surprise, she returned a few days later. I immediately leaped to my feet and approached the door. She greeted me warmly, and I rubbed against her outstretched hand as she settled in beside me. This time I didn't hesitate to crawl onto her warm lap, and she hugged me lovingly, whispering my name. We were like old friends—soulmates, in fact. I always wondered how the other cats selected their humans, but I now knew without a doubt that I wanted to live in her home.

After a while, the other woman approached, and the two conversed softly. I held my breath, willing them to take me away to my fabled forever home. Then, to my great delight, they presented me with a small portable room equipped with a fresh towel and holes in the sides for me to gaze out of. I nervously climbed aboard, as I had seen other cats do on numerous occasions, and waited anxiously to arrive at my new residence.

It was the best choice I ever made, and within a single day, I was transformed from a scared kitty pacing a small cell with an old, worn towel, a single toy, and some dry kibble to the ruler of a massive palace with several rooms, many high ledges, abundant windows, cozy beds, a stack of assorted food, and a box full of toys. My new forever home was everything I had dreamed of and more. I felt like a new cat, and my spirits soared as I basked in the affection and love from my new humans.

Family Tree

I'll be the first to admit that sharing has never been one of my strengths, and after many years of being lovingly cared for by Mom and Grandma, I have actually gotten worse at it. Generally, I claim everything in sight as mine and deny any requests to borrow or use my personal belongings. Mom and Grandma are the rare exceptions to the rule because they love me unconditionally and would never intentionally damage anything that brings me joy. Mom also doesn't eat the same kind of food that I do, so there is minimal risk of her raiding my stash of chicken treats. She always makes space for me on the couch, on her lap, and in my bed, which she seems to think is her bed. We have a fair system worked out, and she has free reign of my house.

When Mom started bringing the man around, I was extremely skeptical. Of course, I was friendly to him and made a point of looking absolutely adorable when he visited. This was a clever act of deception so he would let his guard down and never suspect that I had ulterior motives. I diligently sniffed him from head to toe and inspected him carefully for any signs of illness or other imperfections that might be of concern. He passed my initial screening and appeared fairly harmless. Nonetheless, I continued my careful study of his behavior for many months, wanting to learn all that I could about this newcomer.

He seemed clean and, to my relief, was housetrained. If he wasn't housebroken, then we would have sent him back to wherever he came from because I'm not prepared to deal with that challenge. He never tried to use my litter box and seemed to understand that it was off-limits. The man preferred plant-based food, which I despised, and he showed no interest in my meals. This was also a point in his favor, as I did not want to start worrying about protecting my kibble.

The man exhibited several useful skills, like being able to work the locking mechanism on my canned food, having the strength to open the cold box, also known as a refrigerator, where my open cans are stored, and possessing the dexterity to tear into treat bags and serve a few tasty morsels from the palm of his hand. He preferred to be awake late into the night and sleep the morning away, making him a decent companion once Mom was out of bed for the day. He also enjoyed long afternoon naps, which are right up my alley.

On the other hand, the man came with some downsides. He is much larger than Mom and wanted to claim half of my bed, which I adamantly protested. I made a point of walking back and forth across his chest at night to express my annoyance at not having received a formal written request before he encroached on my space. There are protocols to follow around here, and he ignored all of them. He started putting his personal items atop the nightstand, which created clutter and interfered with me sitting in one of my favorite spots. To remedy this, I began pushing his things onto the floor, taking great satisfaction in hearing them clatter against the hardwood. The noise would jar him awake at night, and after a while, he learned to leave his things on the ground for their own safety. Placing them back on the nightstand would just necessitate me shoving them off again and waking everyone up a second time.

It has been several months now, and the man and I have come to an understanding. He is permitted to freely roam the house, but I still assert my dominance from time to time by challenging him for space or clearing his belongings off of surfaces. Sometimes, I do it just for fun.

The man introduced me to two furry beasts, which I have learned are called dogs, with sandy-colored coats, floppy ears, stinky breath, and friendly dispositions. Again, he failed to file the proper paperwork before bringing them to my home, but by that point, I was all too familiar with his careless ways. I'll admit that I was startled when they came barreling through my door unannounced and with reckless disregard for privacy and personal space. They neglected to knock like everyone else does when requesting entry to my estate. What if I had been using the litter box or having a particularly personal conversation with Ms. Fish?

One of them had shaggy fur, a long tail that sometimes cleared off surfaces more efficiently than I did, and a limp that resulted in an off-kilter gait. She had experienced a difficult life with her first family before coming to join us in my happy home. I never asked about the old injury, but she seemed content and was still mobile with the use of just three legs. While I was initially upset at the intrusion and the fact that she occupied so much floor space, I had to respect her for maintaining a positive attitude despite the adversity in her life.

The other dog was smaller and stockier, with a skinny tail and a timid disposition. At our first meeting, she cowered by the door, and Mom had to coax her into the house. I was observing from the safety of my climbing tower and appreciated the courtesy she showed by not charging in and crowding my space the way her twin did. She often stared anxiously at the ground and would shake with fear in my presence. When I drew near, she would freeze and try to blend into the surroundings.

She had difficulty crossing thresholds and would stand meekly in doorways or in places where the floor changed color or texture, seemingly glued to the spot and unable to handle the division. Mom and the man would encourage her to enter the room and disregard the invented barrier, but she struggled with this concept. I could never understand what gave her such pause, as I easily moved from room to room with no hesitation or issue traversing different floor textures. She would watch me stroll into the bedroom while she remained suspended in animation, peering in at me nervously. After careful consideration and observation of her habits, I also attributed this behavior to a rough puppyhood and was glad she now had someone to love and care for her.

I initially resisted the intrusion and gave these newcomers a wide berth, just in case they were putting on a skillful ruse and intended to eat me in my sleep. They were not very coordinated and would slosh their water over the side of the bowl, creating a dangerous splash zone that I was careful to avoid. They crunched their food loudly and hopped about, flailing those long tails, when Mom or the man would pick up the colorful ropes the dogs wore to go outside. They were always so excited for these recurring outings, and I wondered what brief tasks they attended to three times a day. I later learned the truth and am still horrified by the idea.

I've never fully come to terms with having the dogs in my residence and sharing some of Mom's attention, but they have learned to respect my personal space and have proven to be more trainable than Mom or the man. They are too docile for home protection purposes; however, they would make excellent additions to my mouse toy army, given their size and strength. Alas, some creatures lack the proper dispositions for military prowess.

Today, I consider the beasts and their man to be acceptable acquaintances, and at some point, they may graduate to second-tier family members. Mom and Grandma are my only immediate family, and honestly, I'm not sure that I need anyone else. Our house is a happy one, and surprisingly, I can no longer imagine life without the man and dogs.

The Battle for Water

The night is still, and Mom and the man are resting peacefully in my bed. I am perched on the nightstand, debating what to do with my free time until breakfast is served. I could conduct another perimeter check to ensure all is well in my territory, but I recently patrolled the area and have no reason to believe there are any threats in the vicinity. I could spend time with Mousey and Ms. Fish, who are both lounging on the floor near my climbing tower, but Mousey and I are disagreeing over whether he is allowed in my tower when I'm not there. The debate became heated this afternoon, and I'm giving him the silent treatment as punishment.

I gaze down at Mom, watching the sheets rise and fall with each breath. My eyes drift to the two water cups beside me, which Mom dutifully fills to the brim each night for my convenience. There was a time when we would drink from the same cup, but

I would get annoyed if the water level became too low for me to reach without having to shove my face into the cup. That just messes up my artfully groomed whiskers and results in me getting my nose wet, which is completely untenable. We ultimately decided that she should use a separate cup.

I sniff at my cup, then at hers, and then at mine again. To my astonishment, there is a piece of fur floating in my cup. Mom must attend to this immediately, as I should not be forced to drink tainted water. I need a bell to wake her up whenever necessary or for general summoning purposes when she's in another room. This would be much more convenient than having to walk around the house, locate her, and lead her to whatever task needs immediate attention.

I stare at the strand of floating fur with dismay, feeling incredibly unsettled by these unsanitary conditions. I could try to fish it out with my paw, but that would require me to touch the water, and that is not a viable option. Mom's cup is only partially full, and I face the previously mentioned water level issue if I choose to drink from that vessel. I could jump down, wander out to the living room, hop onto the large chest of drawers where my food and water dishes are housed, and drink from there. That dish is untouched following the refill at dinner; however, it's so far away and the short trek would require more effort than I'm currently willing to muster.

Then I spot the man's cup resting atop the nightstand on the opposite side of the bed. Eagerly, I tromp across the pillows, stepping right over the man's head. Mom shifts slightly from the disturbance, but the man lies still. I carefully assess his cup and find that it's full to the brim. There are no stray hairs or other debris to be seen, which pleases me immensely. It passes inspection, and I'm just about to take a dainty sip when I hear the man whisper something.

I freeze and slowly turn to face him. He's watching me closely, and I'm disappointed in myself for not being stealthier. We stare at each other intently for a moment, and then I casually begin to sniff the other items on the nightstand as though I was simply having a look around. This puts him at ease, and he nestles deeper into the sheets.

A minute passes, and I check to ensure that his eyes are closed. I wish he would roll over so he wasn't facing me, but he appears to be fast asleep. Satisfied, I crouch down beside the cup, accidentally shifting one of the other items crowding the surface of the nightstand. Horrified by my clumsiness, I cringe at the sound of movement. The man's hand darts out and covers the opening of the cup. I stare at it for a second before standing to my full height and glaring down at him. He holds my gaze and whispers something more forcefully.

Now I'm annoyed. Given that I have claimed everything in this house as my own, this is my cup, and he is only borrowing it to store water overnight. Therefore, if I'm thirsty, then I have first dibs on the cup and its contents. This is just common sense, and he seems to be struggling with the simple concept.

What to do now? I could challenge him to a duel, but he's bigger than me, and I don't want to take my chances in a physical altercation. I could retreat to the other side of the bed and resign myself to the tainted water, but that's disgusting. I shift my weight from paw to paw, my eyes still locked on the man.

Finally, I turn my back and march to the opposite side of the nightstand, feigning indifference. I stare at the ground and then into the closet, where my secret hideout room is located, debating my next move. I suspect that if I keep this up for a few minutes, he will drift off again, leaving the water unprotected.

I hear a rustling sound behind me, but I am determined not to show any interest. Silence settles over the room, and I wait patiently. There's no real rush, and the night is young.

I risk a peek over my shoulder. The man has rolled onto his back and appears serene. His mouth is slightly open, and he begins to breathe noisily.

Slowly, I turn around, being careful not to disturb any of the other items strewn about and make the same mistake twice.

There is a small piece of paper covering the cup, and I chuckle to myself at the feeble attempt to create a barrier. This is no obstacle, and I know exactly what to do. I reach out and gently tap the paper, causing it to slide partially off. I repeat this several times until it tips off its perch and flutters to the ground. Without pausing, I lean down and begin to lap up the water, feeling incredibly superior for solving this amateur puzzle so quickly.

As I'm congratulating myself, the man suddenly sits up, snatches the cup away, and kicks off the sheets. I'm temporarily stunned and have never seen him exhibit such speed and agility at this time of night. He slides out of bed, and the movement rouses Mom. Removing the eye covering she wears to block out any light, she murmurs something groggily and glances back and forth between us.

I tilt my head slightly and give her an innocent look, pretending like I have no idea what is happening. There is no way I could possibly be responsible for all of this commotion.

The man says a few words and ambles out of the room. I hear the sound of water running, followed by some banging in the kitchen. For a moment, I wonder if he could be preparing an early breakfast to appease me. No, that seems unlikely given the tension between us right now. I hold my position and wait for his next move.

He returns shortly, shakes his head, pats me lightly, and places a different kind of cup on the nightstand. He collapses back into bed and burrows under the covers.

I examine the new container closely and find that there is only a tiny opening on the top. It's too small for me to dunk my paw into, not that I really want to employ that tactic. This momentarily stumps me, and I sit back to consider the problem. The man learned from the paper barrier failure and has constructed a much trickier system this time. I place my paw on the container and press down, hoping the top will collapse under my weight, but it doesn't budge. Knowing it will be fruitless, I try to wedge my nose and mouth into the small opening to ensure that I've tested all options.

My frustration is mounting, and I give the man a piercing stare. How can he sleep soundly in my bed when he has gravely disrespected me and violated my rights to the water? There must be consequences for his actions so this kind of behavior doesn't become a habit.

Looking back down at the cup, then at the edge of the nightstand, and then back at the cup, I hatch the perfect plan for revenge. If I could laugh maniacally, I would. I reach out with one paw and slide the container toward the edge closest to the bed. It makes a light scraping noise, and I pause, but the man doesn't stir this time. Clearly, he has a false sense of security, and I need to address that immediately. I push the container again, and one side now hangs precariously over the edge. My tail twitches in anticipation, and I feel a sense of pride at my clever plan. With one final tap, I send the container tumbling down to the ground with a bang. A stream of water arcs through the air, and I leap back to avoid contact. Unfortunately, my aim is off, and the liquid splatters harmlessly on the floor instead of splashing all over the man.

The noise startles him and Mom, and they sit up abruptly, looking bewildered and concerned. I realize now that I should have fled the scene to avoid suspicion, but I wanted a front-row seat for my revenge and hadn't planned that far ahead. Now they're both staring at me, and Mom speaks in an irritated tone and snaps her fingers in my direction.

This has a surprising effect on me, and I feel ashamed and guilty because my intention was not to annoy her. She's my favorite person in the whole world. I notice that the container wedged itself right side up between the bed and the nightstand so most of the water did not spill. The guilty feeling disappears.

The man fishes the container out of the crevice and places it on the floor, which is a smart decision. Mom rises to her feet, picks up my cup, and plods toward the kitchen. I drop to the ground and trot after her. She dumps out the old water, washes out the cup, refills it, and replaces it on the nightstand.

I hop up to inspect the cup and find that it's full to the brim and fur-free, which is perfect. I lap greedily at the cool water, congratulating myself on a job well done. When I've had my fill, I step lightly onto the bed and curl up against Mom's side. She embraces me gently, and we fall asleep in each other's arms.

This is My Pillow

My nights generally follow a similar pattern. First, I knead Mom's arm until my legs and paws grow tired. Then I plaster myself against her side before drifting off into a satisfying nap. When I wake up and need to change positions, I wander over to the second pillow and curl up with my legs tucked beneath me and my tail wrapped protectively around my body. I enjoy watching Mom sleep and find her presence soothing. If I need something, I can wake her up by simply stretching out a paw and pressing it against her cheek, which is very convenient.

Tonight, I'm lounging on the second pillow, gazing at Mom and wondering why she sleeps for only one extended period every day instead of taking a series of short naps like I do. It also seems odd that she wakes up to a screeching sound that emanates from a shiny, black rectangle, which is called a phone if you haven't seen one before. When the annoying noise begins, she touches the phone to quiet it and attempts to fall back asleep before the sound echoes through the room again. This ritual seems to annoy her, and I don't understand why she doesn't silence the device permanently by burying it outside where it won't disturb us anymore.

The noise rouses her every day and announces that it's time for breakfast. Now that I think about it, maybe I can live with the unsettling screeching sound that rings in the morning.

The man has a very unusual sleep pattern, staying up late into the night and waking long after the sun has risen. I believe he shares my affinity for the cover of darkness. There is something so alluring and mysterious about the night. Once Mom is out of bed for the day, I can snuggle up to the man if I feel so inclined and enjoy a luxurious morning nap.

As I'm considering whether he and I may share other similarities, he opens the door and wanders into the room. I notice that all of the lights in the house are off, which means he is preparing for sleep. He heads toward the side of the bed where I am currently lounging and pulls the sheets back. I look up at him and have no intention of conceding my cozy position. He is welcome to lie close to me, but I am currently using this pillow, and that is not up for debate.

The man eases himself down onto the soft mattress and slowly reclines toward my pillow. He glances over his shoulder to see if I'm moving, but I have no interest in going anywhere. He leans a bit closer and checks for a reaction, but I'm not giving in and intend to call his bluff. He's not going to actually lie on me because that would be unacceptable, and Mom would surely scold him. I twitch one ear in mild annoyance at this game.

He leans back further and is now almost touching me. There is a pause as he again waits for me to make a move. I decline to engage and simply watch him with interest. Then he does the unthinkable. He lets his head gently graze my back. I hold completely still, determined to win this standoff. The seconds tick by as we both hope the other will concede. To prove that I'm totally unbothered by this, I sniff his hair and let my whiskers tickle his forehead. He makes a soft sound in response and says my name. I shift a bit as he lets his head partially rest on me.

"Look man," I say silently. "I was here first. This is my pillow, and I'm currently using it. That means you can't use it. Just move over and sleep without the pillow tonight."

He doesn't respond and instead relaxes so the weight of his head is more fully resting on me. I'm feeling crowded and confined with this current setup and realize that I must admit defeat or risk being slowly crushed. We'll face off at the same time and place tomorrow.

I stand abruptly, displacing his head and catching him off guard. I'm fully awake now and feel refreshed after my nap. My irritation is quickly replaced by curiosity.

With sudden energy, I leap to the floor and sprint out of the room, skidding around the corner at full speed and catapulting myself onto the kitchen table. This vantage point offers a great view of the room, and I spot Ms. Fish with her blue and white feather tail. I launch an aerial assault and snatch her up in my jaws before racing to the other side of the room and climbing to the top of my tower to gaze out the window.

Each night, Mom closes the thin blinds that cover the window and prevent me from seeing out. While this is inconvenient, I have learned to stick one paw in between the slats and create a small void to peer through. I toss Ms. Fish from the tower because I want it all to myself for midnight spying endeavors. Then I create a peephole in the slats and gaze out at the dark night.

There is limited activity tonight, and not a single person or animal is in sight. Even the noisy transportation boxes that rumble down the street seem to have been put to bed. This is disappointing because I had hoped to catch someone in a compromising position and add a few pages to my blackmail file. You never know when a bit of leverage will come in handy. I want to be prepared to use someone's secrets against them at a later date.

After a few minutes, I grow bored and feel my energy waning. I release my hold on the blinds, which snap back into place, and hop noiselessly to the ground. I pad into the bedroom and resume my former position tucked up against Mom's side. It's time for another nap.

Intruder

There is something rather satisfying about owning land. The second we moved into this place, I claimed everything in sight as mine, and no one has ever dared to challenge that claim. I feel safe and secure here, and it's nice not to worry about any strangers using my things when my back is turned.

Anytime Mom has guests over, I inspect them at the door to ensure that they are friends and not foes. I have a strict policy that prohibits suspicious people or beasts from crossing my threshold. Generally, she associates with decent people, but one can never be too careful, and I only want the best for her.

I worry about Mom's safety and have tried on numerous occasions to demonstrate techniques to ward off invaders. Just last week, Mousey helped me showcase some lethal moves that involved tossing your opponent high into the air, slamming them on the ground, and chewing on their tail. I accidentally swallowed a few strands of his purple fur in the process, but I don't think it detracted from the lesson. Mousey was more than willing to play the attacker in the simulation, never once complaining about being tired or a bit bruised.

Mom watched closely as I repeated the moves a few times. However, when it came time for her to practice the maneuvers, she seemed not to have retained the valuable lesson. I stood back to let her face off with Mousey, who obligingly held his position, but she just gently scratched my head and gingerly placed Mousey on top of the climbing tower.

"No, no, no!" I meowed in exasperation. "Put him back on the ground and try that body slam move I showed you. This is for your own safety."

She failed to grasp the importance of the training session and refused to attempt a single maneuver. I decided to try again later.

Today I'm working on a lesson plan to approach the problem from a new angle. Perhaps because Mousey is so much smaller than I am, Mom didn't understand that he was supposed to be a threat in the demonstration. Maybe I need a more formidable foe as my assistant. I'll have to review some resumes and assess potential candidates.

I'm busy ticking through the necessary qualifications in my head when I hear an ominous sound. My ears swivel toward it, and my eyes scan the room, searching for the source. I climb silently to my feet and tiptoe cautiously along the wall, unsure if the noise indicates that danger is afoot. All is quiet now, and that feels even more unnerving.

"Show yourself, you coward!" I shout menacingly, hoping to scare any intruder into submission without a fight. "You don't stand a chance against my sharp claws and teeth."

The buzzing sound begins again, and this time I spot the culprit. A small winged invader is whizzing through the air above the couch, and I can't tell if it's preparing for battle or trying to flee in confusion. I think it's best to assume the worst-case scenario and prepare for a physical altercation.

I feel the fur on the back of my neck stand on end as I trot forward to engage the threat. The buzzing beast ignores my approach and continues circling without any clear direction. Once within pouncing range, I pause and wait until it meanders in my general direction. Seizing the opportunity, I launch myself through the air, swinging my paws wildly and trying to knock the menace to the ground. I intend to pin it to the couch or the wall and smash it beneath my paws.

Unfortunately, the fiend executes evasive maneuvers and slips through my grasp, flying right over my head. I land gracefully on the back of the couch and whirl around for a second attempt before it has time to retaliate. I spring into the air, facing the buzzing creature head-on. This time my paw connects with the target, and I feel a sudden sense of accomplishment. However, when I land back on the couch, the critter is no longer beneath my paw. Drat! This adversary is swift and crafty. It seems well-versed in combat, and I suspect it intends to wear me down and switch from defense to offense once I am tired and slow.

I have to do something quickly. This reckless bandit will not get the better of me, and it certainly will not threaten Mom. No one messes with her on my watch.

The assassin has changed course and is now hovering in midair between the couch and the front door. Unfortunately, it's out of my range, and I contemplate the problem for a moment, never taking my eyes off it. The buzzing sound feels like a smug taunt, and rage begins to bubble up within me. I will emerge victorious.

Suddenly, the front door swings open, and the man casually strolls inside, oblivious to the security breach we are facing. The pesky foreign agent whizzes right past him into the afternoon sunshine and disappears. I'm relieved that the threat has been removed, but I'm also disappointed that I missed my chance to stomp it into submission. I was really looking forward to that gleeful moment. Ah well, there will be other opportunities.

The man notices me perched precariously on the extreme edge of the couch and wanders over to stroke the top of my head. I nudge his hand in appreciation and gaze into his eyes, seeing him in a new light.

"Good teamwork!" I declare. "With your size and my superior intellect, we can defend this turf from any foe. I will allow you to use the second pillow tonight as a reward for your assistance."

Betrayal

I am incredibly loyal and committed to my family, which consists of Mom and Grandma. The man is now in contention for admission into the family, but I haven't made up my mind yet. For now, he remains in the favored acquaintance category along with the two sandy-furred dogs.

I don't know what I would do without Mom. She feeds me, plays with me, provides fresh water, acts as a heating pad at night, and showers me with love and compliments. No one else knows exactly how I like my food prepared, how to pour water into the bathtub so it doesn't touch my paws, allowing me to lap it up at my convenience, or where to find my lost toys. Mom provides invaluable services on a daily basis.

The man acts as a surrogate for Mom when she is not home or is otherwise unavailable. He is being trained in the art of serving me and is slowly catching on. I'll admit that he makes an effort, but no one can rival Mom's skill and attention to detail.

Then there are the two dogs that were part of the package when the man moved into my residence. I find them amusing, and they are somewhat trainable, although there is a communication barrier. They are not very useful as servants, but they seem to follow my instructions and have never encroached on my food or water. I consider them harmless, submissive subjects that generally abide by my rules and regulations.

I am the most intelligent, handsome, and interesting cat in the world, but I still enjoy surrounding myself with loyal subjects that regularly display their adoration and respect. Someone must rule the world, and it should certainly be me.

Speaking of loyal subjects and family, Mom notices that I'm gazing up at the open bedroom window, but I lack a comfortable perch in the vicinity. She scurries away and returns a moment later with a comfy chair from the other room, demonstrating her strength and stamina. Once it's correctly positioned, I hop onto the seat, stretch my front paws up to the window ledge, and balance gracefully on my back paws.

I can see everything from this vantage point. Warm air drifts over me, bringing unfamiliar scents that I take a moment to catalog and analyze. The sun is shining, and everything is so alive and vibrant. The world is a noisy place, and my sensitive ears pick up a host of intriguing sounds. I am captivated.

I wonder where the fish, chickens, turkeys, and ducks that eventually end up in my bowl live. It must be close by so they can hop into the wet food cans whenever they're ripe, or maybe I should say when they're mature. I'm not sure what the correct terminology is for a food-ready duck. I never see them strolling around outside; however, since I don't know what they look like, they would be difficult to recognize. This concerns me, and I add it to my mental to-do list. Tomorrow, I will figure out what a duck looks like.

There is a transparent mesh covering stretched across the window that prevents me from jumping through it to explore the mysterious world beyond my home. A part of me wants to venture forth and have grand adventures while I map out an expanded territory. I'm sure I would meet many interesting characters along the way, and it would certainly be a new experience to live without the confines of these walls.

The other part of me is afraid to leave the safety of my home, given water falls from the sky, I have yet to see any food bowls lying around, and there are so many unfamiliar humans and beasts about, some of whom might prove to be unfriendly. It's probably safer to observe my subjects from a distance.

Just a few feet beyond the window, there is a path carved through the lush greenery. Humans seem to enjoy strolling this route, and they often have dogs tethered to their hands. The dogs seem less content to walk within the defined boundaries of the path and instead choose to meander around the grassy area with their noses hovering inches above the ground.

Dogs come in all shapes and sizes, but they all appear to respect their people, and I admire this level of training. A dog with long black fur and a fluffy tail wanders by, dragging its human off the path. I wonder what people have against the leafy patches and why they prefer to remain on the sidewalk. The furry creature then squats, and I realize it's about to poop in full view of everyone. That's disgusting! Does it not have any dignity and a desire for privacy?

"Excuse me! No one wants to watch you do that. This is why we all have sandboxes at home," I call out while trying not to look.

The creature doesn't respond, and I alternate between averting my eyes, trying to appear completely horrified, and periodically peeking to check if the beast is leaving. Unfortunately, the wind is blowing in my direction, and a wretched stench wafts over me. I scrunch up my nose and shake my head.

Life by Pumpkin: A Cat's Tale

When the unsanitary act is complete, the beast tries to wander off, but its human produces a small bag and dutifully collects the smelly parcel. I appreciate the attempt to erase all traces of the offensive behavior, but I would hate to have that dirty job. Once the area is cleared of hazardous waste, they continue their walk as though nothing was amiss. I know what happened here today, and I will judge that dog harshly when I inevitably see it strolling through the neighborhood again.

Suddenly, I hear a familiar voice and hone in on it to determine the location. I can't tell what he's saying, but the man is definitely talking to someone outside. I don't recognize the other voice, but I can tell that they're headed in this direction.

My heart sinks when I realize that he is slowly wandering the path in the company of a strange dog and an unfamiliar man. The dog seems comfortable around him, and the man playfully scratches its back. The strange beast wags its tail, much like my golden-furred companions do when they are pet.

This is the worst form of betrayal. The man has a secret second family and has been fraternizing with this strange dog. He should be spending those precious minutes with me and my four-legged sisters, but instead, he is lavishing attention on an outsider. How could he do this to us? I can't believe

I considered upgrading him to the family category of my social circle.

The three of them pause in front of my residence, and I can't tear my gaze away. The strange beast licks the man's hand, and he rewards it by rubbing the top of its head. He then shows it a greenish ball, and the dog barks excitedly, hopping about in an embarrassing display of unchecked joy. The man tosses the ball, and the creature darts away, snatches up the toy in its jaws, and sprints back to drop it at the man's feet. This process is repeated several times while the two men chat amiably. The game has simple rules and is clearly meant for lesser beings than myself. I would soon grow bored with the repetition and lack of strategy involved.

I am appalled by the man's behavior. He doesn't make any attempt to hide his treason and instead seems to flaunt it by playing this childish game in front of everyone. I watch carefully and mentally add the details of this moment to the blackmail files I meticulously maintain.

I will have to cook up an appropriate punishment and alert our dogs that they have competition. If he thinks he can get away with this and deceive us all, he is sadly mistaken.

After a few minutes of this unsettling display of affection for the unfamiliar beast, the man waves goodbye to his friend, gives the dog one last back scratch, and wanders away. I am frozen in place, contemplating my next move. I was unprepared for this scenario, and I hate to be caught off guard. This annoys me almost as much as the betrayal.

I hear the front door open, and it jolts me out of my trance. I drop to the floor and trot into the other room as the man ambles in, seemingly unconcerned that he could have been observed in his treachery. The heightened emotions make me restless, and I leap up to perch on the corner of the kitchen table. I can better assert dominance from a high vantage point, and I fix him with a withering stare.

"I know what you've done. Do you really think you can saunter in here like nothing happened and expect us to continue tolerating your presence?" I think wickedly. "I will not have you embarrassing this family by gallivanting all over town with strangers."

He doesn't understand the wrath he is about to face and calmly removes his foot coverings, causing the laces to wiggle around enticingly. Then he greets our two dogs with an enthusiasm that now disgusts me. They are overjoyed at the attention and exhibit unbridled love and affection for him.

"Stop that! He doesn't deserve your devotion," I inform them. "I saw him lavishing attention on another dog that rubbed against him and licked his hand. Clearly, he has violated our trust."

The dogs don't pay any attention to my warning and continue wagging their tails and hopping about eagerly. I am dismayed at being unable to present a united front to discipline the man.

He catches sight of me observing the happy homecoming from a distance and strides over, smiling innocently. He extends the hand that was recently licked by the strange beast, and I remain stoic. He better not touch me without washing the unfamiliar smell off his skin. I lift my nose to gingerly sniff his fingers and confirm that the stranger's scent is indeed potent. I turn my head away in contempt.

The man proceeds into the kitchen and, to my surprise, cleanses his hands in the water. This is a human process that always disturbs me. They seem to enjoy getting wet, which is my worst nightmare. I shiver at the thought of water on my beautiful fur.

My ears perk up at a crinkling sound, and I swivel my gaze toward the food stash on the other side of the room. The man returns, extends his fist, and opens his fingers, revealing a small quantity of my favorite treats. He no longer smells of the other dog and is now perfumed with chicken.

I want to turn away and reject the offering, but I do love these chicken morsels. Who wouldn't? They are little packets of deliciousness meant to bring joy to the world. They are crunchy on the outside and chewy on the inside. My mouth waters, and with trepidation, I lean forward to inspect them. The temptation is too great, and I gobble them up greedily. I suppose it's some consolation for this whole ordeal, and if I didn't accept the offering, then he, the dogs, or Mousey might eat them, and I can't allow that.

The man speaks softly to me and gently strokes my cheek. This gesture is soothing, and I close my eyes for a moment, feeling temporarily appeased by the food and attention. When he pulls back, I sigh and glance up at him.

"Can I have a few more treats?" I ask. "I'll let you stay if you bring me another handful."

Space-Time Continuum

Mom is busy hanging a shiny, reflective rectangle on the back of the bedroom door. She keeps stepping away, assessing it, and then reaching out to tweak its position. Meanwhile, I am perched on the edge of the nightstand, tilting my head from side to side and trying to figure out what the end goal is. This new addition to the room seems like an unnecessary hassle for very little gain.

"It's slightly off-center," I offer, trying to help with the process. "Shift it half a paw to the right, or maybe that direction is to the left. I can never keep those two straight, but it's definitely half a paw away from perfection."

I don't know why we need this object. Its usefulness is not immediately evident to me, and in my opinion, it disrupts the symmetry of the door. Mom seems fascinated with it and is intent on getting the alignment correct. I'm far less interested because it isn't food, doesn't look like a toy, and can't be used for napping purposes. If she laid it flat on the floor and placed a blanket on top, it might be a different story.

Satisfied with the current position, she nods her head, fixes her hair, and wanders into the adjacent room. I sit quietly for a while, evaluating the new addition to our décor. It's fine, I suppose, but I didn't approve of a redecoration, and I like to be kept informed before any decisions are made that might affect my happiness and well-being.

Given this object appears to be a permanent fixture, I might as well determine if it has any merits. I approach slowly, letting my eyes travel over every inch, and search for secret compartments that might be used for food storage. The hanging rectangle is flat and boring, but it is very shiny.

I rise to my back paws, brace my front paws against the door, and feel it give way with my weight. It swings closed with a soft click. Again, I plant my front paws securely on the door, raise my head to sniff the white border of the new décor, and take a closer look at this shiny object. It appears to be completely unremarkable, which is disappointing.

I shift toward the center of the door and jump back when I realize that another cat is looking straight at me from just inches away. I retreat to a safe distance and glance warily over my shoulder to see if the cat is following me. My heart is racing, and I prepare for a scuffle. The shiny surface looks serene again, but I now know that there is a hidden room, much like this one, embedded within the object.

This development confuses me, so I take a step back, trying to decide how this is possible. Where did this new room come from, and who is the cat living in it? This defies the laws of the universe. Before today, I would've said that the door was simply a flat, uninteresting surface, but Mom has created an entire room inside of it. I don't know how space and physics work, but this is a complex puzzle that I may lack the expertise to solve.

I sit quietly for a moment, staring intently at the suspicious rectangle and waiting for something to happen. It remains unchanged, and there are no signs of life.

It seems that this is going to be my new research project. I must learn more about the unique properties of the glassy surface. Any good scientist would start by making predictions, then assess those theories through careful observation and testing, and finally draw informed conclusions.

Okay, starting with predictions. I pause for a moment, considering what I've discovered so far. The object itself doesn't seem sentient, but it houses a living being, so it must contain more square footage than it would appear to the casual observer. No cat could fit in the narrow space that it occupies, which means it must be a portal to another world. I imagine it's a gap in the space-time continuum that has manifested a window into another realm or possibly just the adjacent house, but another realm sounds much more exciting.

I approach the portal cautiously, wary of the other cat hiding inside. It seemed as frightened of me as I was of it, but I don't take chances with strangers. The room remains quiet as I draw closer, and the cat does not appear. I listen for any suspicious sounds, but the only noise is coming from Mom banging around in the kitchen, which is distracting while I'm trying to conduct a controlled study of this bizarre gateway.

Nervous energy wells up within me, and I shift from paw to paw a few feet from the door. I consider turning back and hiding under the bed, where I know it's safe, but my curiosity and the potential for a valuable scientific discovery take priority. If I have indeed uncovered a new realm that challenges the laws of physics, I must quickly stake my claim to the discovery and then publish my findings. This will ensure that I am remembered in the history books as a great thinker and a bold explorer.

Mustering my courage, I cautiously approach the portal, ready to flee at any moment if something evil is lurking within. Pressing my front paws against the door, I again peer into the glassy surface and come face-to-face with the resident cat. I duck and prepare for an assault from above if it decides to vault through the opening. Nothing happens, and with growing curiosity, I peek through the transparent gateway. The strange cat is there again, gazing at me warily. My heart races, and I try to take even breaths, keep a level head, and make optimal decisions as the situation evolves. Portal Cat seems skittish and not aggressive, which boosts my confidence. I relax a bit, and Portal Cat also appears more at ease.

I feel awkward as we stare at each other, so I lean in and try to sniff my new companion. Portal Cat does the same, but when we are nearly touching noses, I connect with a firm barrier. Reeling back, I see a tiny smudge where my nose touched the shimmery surface. Hmm, this invisible force field must be similar to the ones that keep me from leaping through windows. I try pressing one paw against the barrier, and Portal Cat mimics my movement. We're again met with resistance. I attempt a more aggressive tactic and repeatedly pound my paws against the force field. It remains intact and causes a thumping sound as it is battered against the door.

Portal Cat is keeping pace with me and obediently following my lead. When I press, it presses back; when I sniff, it sniffs; and when I pound my paws, it pounds as well. I'm starting to like this new acquaintance. We might have more in common than I would have guessed, given it's likely from another realm or a parallel universe. I hope that it doesn't try to take credit for the hard work I'm doing to solve this mystery. I suppose it can claim our discovery in its own universe, but I have first dibs on the fame and fortune sure to follow in mine.

I pause the experimentation to make a few mental notes about my findings. The barrier seems immovable, and there are no visible breaks. It appears to prevent both of us from crossing into the other's realm and blocks all scents and sounds. From what I can observe, it is not spreading or receding and remains stable. I don't believe that the gateway presents an imminent threat, and the resident cat seems friendly. The world on the other side looks nearly identical to mine and appears calm and serene.

The door suddenly opens, and Mom pokes her head in. The thumping noise has alerted her that something is afoot. I don't know if I should tell her that I've discovered the portal she installed. She must know what it is, but I'm not sure if the mystical properties are supposed to be a secret. Satisfied that I haven't caused any damage, she retreats to the kitchen.

I pad over to the door again and nudge it closed. I need to mull over my findings and then determine the next steps in my research. I rise onto my back paws and again come face-to-face with Portal Cat.

"Should we meet back here at the same time tomorrow and conduct a few more tests?" I ask, hoping it can read facial expressions since I don't think it can hear me. It just stares back at me curiously. "You'll definitely come back, right? There's so much I want to know about you."

Eventually, I give a slight nod, and my companion does the same. Wow, we really are on the same page. It's almost scary how quickly we learned each other's ways. Portal Cat seems adept at following directions, and I think this could be the start of a beautiful new friendship.

Rescue Mission

My toys hold a special place in my heart. They play valuable roles in my life, and each has a unique skill set and personality. Even though I slowly tear the less durable ones to pieces, I do it all out of love. I'm sure they understand that their sole mission is to serve me and ensure my happiness. There is some danger involved, given I sometimes play rough. I was born with these long ivory claws and spear-like teeth, and sometimes I get carried away in the heat of the moment.

Mom regularly brings me new toy options, and I take training and assessing the merits of these newcomers very seriously. I immediately put them through their paces and keep careful notes so I know who is best equipped for each activity. Let me introduce you to the major players.

Mousey is small and purple, with a pink nose, a skinny tail, and a silky coat. He has a light, aerodynamic frame that makes him an ideal candidate for my aerial assault squad. I have been running attack simulations with him in case he's ever needed for combat. Mousey responds well to directions and is a loyal recruit whom I can trust with my deepest, darkest secrets. I have promoted him to the rank of general and entrusted him with the supervision and coordination of my other mouse forces. They're all surprisingly similar in size and shape, and I believe most are related to Mousey. The main difference is their fur color. I'll admit that their bright tones really make them stand out in a room, and I would prefer that they have better camouflage in order to effectively sneak up on an enemy.

Playtime with Mousey and his compatriots involves flinging them high into the air from the ground, from my climbing tower, or from another high vantage point. I want them to be familiar with the sensation so they're not afraid and can focus on landing atop and incapacitating the enemy in a real-life scenario. Sometimes, I pin them between my front paws and gnaw on their vibrantly colored tails. This might seem a bit harsh, but I'm toughening them up in case they're ever captured by opposing forces. I can't have them spilling our secrets and revealing the positions of our other troops. Battle is both mentally and physically taxing, and I intend to command the finest battalions in the land.

Life by Pumpkin: A Cat's Tale

Ms. Fish is my therapist. She's blue and white, with a soft frame and a delightful feather tail. I find her presence comforting, and I often enjoy napping with her in my climbing tower after a long afternoon chat. She's a great listener and always gives me her undivided attention. She really understands me, even though we're very different. We occasionally fight, mainly over whether she is allowed in my climbing tower and favorite cardboard box. She can be pushy and doesn't always understand that sometimes I just need alone time to ponder the mysteries of the universe. Ms. Fish will keep trying to climb or hop into the box with me, and I have to repeatedly remove her. After these little spats, we always quickly make up.

Then there is the shiny red bow that I was given on that marvelous day of the year when people open boxes wrapped in crinkly paper. It's by far my favorite day, and I play in the boxes for weeks. I always keep a few ribbons and bows in storage until I receive new ones the next year. It's a wonderful tradition, and I can't understand why humans show little interest in the boxes themselves. That just means that there are more toys for me to enjoy.

Bow is fast and agile, and with a gentle push, she can go careening across the floor. Her sense of direction is lacking, and when we practice chasing down potential enemies, she often veers wildly off course. We're working on her aim and consistency, but I think she has real potential and never seems to tire.

Ball of Yarn is also a favorite of mine because, while he may appear unremarkable as a simple round ball, he can stretch out for what seems like miles and hopelessly tangle enemies in his grasp. I often roll him across the floor, take the end of his tail in my mouth, and run around the room to help him stretch out to his full length and practice snagging the corners of objects to create a complicated string maze. I think it will be a very effective deterrent if we are ever invaded. The problem is that once Ball of Yarn is unrolled and thoroughly tangled, he can't untangle himself and return to his original ball format. He always requires Mom's assistance to wind himself back into a spherical shape. Nevertheless, I value his specialized skill set.

Speaking of Mousey, he is stealthily approaching the climbing tower where I'm bedded down. Mom is crouched beside him and keeps glancing back and forth between us. Mousey continues on his path and reaches the base of the tower. He must be looking to test my defense systems. I rise to my paws to meet this challenge, and my eyes lock onto his furry frame. I think I'm going to enjoy this exercise.

Life by Pumpkin: A Cat's Tale

Silently, he gazes up at me, skitters to one side of the tower, and then launches himself through the air, just like we've practiced. With expert precision and great speed, I swat him out of his flight path, sending him careening toward the hardwood floor below and landing with a hollow thump.

He lies still for a moment, and Mom slides over to check on him. When she gets close, Mousey suddenly rights himself and begins another approach, seemingly undeterred. I crouch down and monitor his progress. He pauses a few feet away, and I prepare myself for another barrage. Sure enough, he executes a flawless aerial attack, but I'm far too swift and easily bat him away. I definitely have a size advantage.

Mousey might think that one day the student will overtake the master, but not in my house. I am the tactical genius who devised our offensive and defensive strategies. I invented the idea of silently sneaking up to the tower and attacking from above. Who does Mousey think he is challenging?

He returns for a third attempt, and I shift my weight to my back paws so the front ones can deliver another swat. Again, Mousey fails to penetrate my defenses, and he goes flying toward the couch.

Adrenaline courses through me, and I leap from my tower in pursuit. I land beside him and issue another whack that sends him spinning across the slick floor. He slides right into the dark void under the couch and disappears. My heart sinks, and I'm suddenly alarmed.

I race forward and peer under the couch, but the space is very narrow, and it's too dark to see anything. I lie on my side and stretch my paws into the chasm, feeling around desperately but failing to reach my target.

"Mousey!" I cry in distress. "Hold on, I'll save you!"

I call for more forces to assemble, create a chain extending into the darkness, and retrieve our lost comrade. I can't believe this is happening. How could I lose my general in a training exercise? Who would take over in Mousey's place? He has no natural successor, and I can't imagine training someone else from scratch. What a disaster.

I am starting to despair because the mouse forces don't immediately follow orders. I continue to feel around beneath the couch with both paws, but Mousey must be wedged too far in to reach. I hope he isn't wounded. We were just practicing, and it wasn't supposed to be a real fight. What if I never get him back?

Mom wanders over and kneels beside me. I look at her desperately, unsure what she can possibly do to help. Her track record in dire situations is second to none, and she's my last hope.

"Please, rescue him. Don't let him perish under there," I plead. "This is all my fault, and I can't bear the idea of Mousey suffering."

Mom seems to understand the situation and lies down on the ground, extending one long arm under the couch. I hold my breath, barely daring to hope, as she reaches to one side and then the other. Slowly, she pulls back, and when her hand emerges from the darkness, I see that Mousey is clutched in her fingers.

My spirits soar, and relief washes over me. She sets Mousey down and brushes some dust from his fur. I appreciate her concern and nuzzle her hand to show my thanks. She massages my neck, and I feel the tense muscles relax.

I carefully scoop Mousey up and retreat to the tower, setting him lightly at my feet. Looking him over, I don't see any obvious injuries. He appears to have emerged unscathed, and the tough little guy isn't even complaining about his encounter with the abyss beneath the couch.

I lie down with him between my front paws, feeling protective of my best soldier. Mom then tucks Ms. Fish beside Mousey, and I beam up at her. She knows that I need someone to talk to, and Ms. Fish always helps me sort through my struggles.

Foodie

I consider myself to be quite a foodie. My diet is incredibly varied because I quickly grow bored if I'm served similar flavors on a regular basis. When that happens, I simply turn up my nose at the breakfast spread Mom has prepared and pretend like I have no idea what I am supposed to do with the bowl of tired, boring mush.

Mom always suggests that I sample it, but if I hold my ground and refuse to engage with the offered sustenance, she will eventually feel guilty and open a different can of food. I've got this system down to a fine science, and Mom is no match for the distressed, hungry look I've mastered for these instances.

Today is one of those days. It's unclear to me why Mom has not learned to anticipate my reaction when she tries to serve the same cuisine two days in a row. I'm hopeful that someday she'll catch on, and we won't have to go through this process anymore. Alas, here we are again.

She's trying to convince me that the blended fish mixture is worthy of my attention. Mom points to the small bowl as if I don't know that it's there. My sense of smell is far superior to hers, and I have a sensitive palate. Obviously, I know that there's food in the bowl, but I am the master of this house, and I demand that she take this inferior offering away and provide me with another option.

"I have a taste for chicken with gravy. Why don't you prepare that dish, and I'll conduct a taste test to decide if it is an acceptable dinner option?" I tell her, licking my lips at the thought of chicken.

She points to the bowl again and murmurs something in an encouraging tone. I don't react and just stare at her blankly. Mom then picks up the bowl and holds it close to my face. I turn my head away in frustration. It is so hard to find good service these days, and I'll need to have a word with the manager of this restaurant.

I turn my back and saunter off toward the kitchen. Sometimes, I literally have to show her what needs to be done. She dutifully trails behind, still carrying the rejected food. I'm well aware that open cans of food are stored in the large white refrigerator, which is unnaturally cold inside. I approach the chilly box and paw at the door. Unfortunately, I haven't figured out how to work the complicated locking system and need Mom to open it for me.

She doesn't immediately react and stands there, watching me. With a sigh, she puts a cover on the old bowl, which is a smart move since I might want that one tomorrow, wrenches open the heavy door, places the bowl inside, and picks up another can. Mom retrieves a clean dish and begins preparing my meal. I watch her with interest because I really am hungry and would like her to hurry up. She adds a tiny bit of water to the bowl, and I hear her mixing it thoroughly so the food is nice and soft, just how I like it. My mouth begins to water, and I hope she has my order right this time.

She carries my breakfast back to the picnic area and places it gently on the white towel used to sop up any spills. I approach it eagerly and am delighted to confirm that it is indeed chicken. Jackpot! I begin to eat ravenously, but suddenly my tongue is greeted with an odd flavor. Hmm, there is something mixed in with the chicken, and I immediately spit it out and gaze down at the bowl. It's round and green, and I am alarmed to discover that there are plants commingled with my chicken.

"What is the meaning of this?" I ask, glaring at Mom. "Why would you spoil perfectly good chicken by adding some disgusting plants? Don't ever do this again."

She continues to watch me and doesn't look at all remorseful for defiling what could have been a delicious meal. I'm too hungry to go through the process of leading her back to the refrigerator a second time and waiting anxiously for her to produce another main course. I'll just have to make do.

I glance back at the bowl and count the little green pieces poking through the sea of finely ground chicken. I also notice suspicious orange chunks and decide that those are unacceptable. Carefully, I begin to lap up the chicken, leaving the green and orange debris behind. This is a painstaking process, but what else can I do in this situation? Clearly, those plants are not supposed to be eaten. I accidentally slurp one of them up and immediately spit it back into the bowl. Gross!

The dish begins to look like some kind of maze, with empty areas situated between the plant scraps. Finally, I've eaten all that I can without having to lick the chicken off the plants. It's a shame to waste that bit, but I think it's the right decision. I step back, lick my lips, and examine the bowl. It resembles a work of modern food art, with colorful chunks strewn about.

"Mom, take my plate away and throw out the rest of that tainted food. I will not be forced to go through this process again," I instruct. "Mom?"

She doesn't immediately react, and I glance over at her, ready to issue a disapproving look. However, she is seated at the table with a plate of her own, which draws my interest. Hmm, this requires further investigation. I always like to inspect her food to ensure that it hasn't spoiled and isn't something that I want to claim for my own meal. She doesn't eat tasty food like I do and instead prefers plants. I don't know how she subsists on this diet or why she doesn't consume meals similar to my own. She has thumbs and knows where to find cans of chicken. None of this makes sense to me.

I leap onto the table and casually stroll toward her, my eyes locked on her meal. Our normal pattern involves me thoroughly sniffing her food, turning up my nose, and losing interest. Generally, she doesn't react when I begin my inspection; however, this time she tries to keep the plate away from me. This is a curious development, and I'm intrigued.

My sensitive nose detects an enticing scent. What exotic treat is she hiding? I inch forward, and she slides the plate away. I advance again, and she shifts as well. This is now a cat-and-mouse game.

"Stop that," I order. "This will be easier for everyone if you just sit still."

There are two circular items slathered in a creamy substance on the plate. It's bagel day, and I want it! It's mine!

Life by Pumpkin: A Cat's Tale

Mom lifts one piece to take a bite, and the distraction provides a brief window of opportunity. I scamper forward, heading for the second piece, which is unguarded. She instinctively lifts her hand to fend off my advance and hunches over the plate protectively. I quickly change course and plant my nose into the slice she's holding. I manage to lick the surface once before she snatches it away, staring at the void I left in the cream cheese. The taste is smooth and rich, and I lick the remnants off my nose with pleasure. This is what I should be served every day.

Mom tears off the area that I touched and begins chowing down on the rest while eyeing me warily. As I approach again, she stands up, which puts the plate far out of my reach. I meow in frustration, and she turns her back. Giving her a pitiful, hungry look to make her feel guilty is now out of the question.

She chews quickly and loudly, and I focus my gaze on the untouched piece. Using my mental superpowers, I attempt to lift it into the air and let it fall to the floor. I concentrate and squint my eyes a bit, but it doesn't appear to be working. I scoot to the very edge of the table and try again. Perhaps I was out of range the first time. My second attempt fails as well, and Mom begins consuming that piece.

Hmm, it seems I've been beaten. If I can't have the lovely cream, then I demand the next best thing.

I hop off the table, feeling full and a bit sleepy, and plod over to my bag of treats. I paw at it, and the package makes a wonderful crinkly sound. This catches Mom's attention, and she wanders over, setting the now empty plate on the table. I paw at the bag again and stare up at her with wide eyes, which she always finds irresistible.

She kneels and gently runs her hand along my back. I close my eyes as she repeats this soothing motion. I rub against Mom's arm, marking her to ensure that she smells like me so all other cats and beasts know that she's mine. Involuntarily, I begin to purr softly and then lie down, enjoying her undivided attention. I love her so much that I temporarily forget about the treats, which never happens.

The sound of the bag rouses me from my meditative state, and I'm instantly alert. Mom pours a few pieces into her hand and offers them to me. I gobble them up happily and lick her palm since there is still some residue on her skin. Feeling very full and satisfied, I amble over to a sunny spot on the floor and flop down on my side for a morning nap. I hope my dreams involve bowls of that creamy spread.

Proper Grooming Etiquette

As ruler of this realm, I regularly assess my strengths and weaknesses. After years of experience governing my loyal subjects, I have concluded that my greatest strengths are my intelligence, my ability to look adorable, and my skill at making others feel guilty for not doing exactly what I say when I say it. No one should ever disobey my direct commands, but sometimes they need a little nudge to comply.

These qualities come naturally to me, as I'm a quick learner and very observant, which allows me to draw informed conclusions and make optimal decisions. I was born with superior intelligence and have honed that ability over the years by taking naps atop scholarly books and letting the knowledge sink in. Self-improvement is very important to me.

I also inherited exceptional genes and have learned to use them to my advantage. My silky orange fur exhibits an aristocratic pattern of stripes, which creates a pleasing contrast to my long white whiskers. I have wide, innocent eyes, a small pink nose, and a perfect set of white teeth. My elegant tail is held high when I walk, swishing gracefully from side to side with the sway of my hips.

I invest countless hours in my appearance and always practice proper hygiene. In order to look my best, I block off time in my busy schedule for grooming at least twice per day. There's nothing worse than a bad hair day, which is why I maintain a regimented bathing schedule.

I begin by thoroughly licking my paws, including between my claws, to remove any dirt and comb my fur. Then I move up my legs, twist at an odd angle to reach my shoulders and sides, and roll onto my back to straighten out the soft fur on my belly.

My face and head are the most challenging since my tongue can't stretch that far. Instead, I lick my paw, reach to the top of my head, and rub back and forth to brush the fur. I repeat this process several times, carefully styling my hair in the latest fashion. The wisps on the top of my ears are the most difficult, and I take my time sculpting them into perfect triangles. Bending my ears forward and running my paws back and forth over the area until my fur cooperates has proven to be a solid strategy. Mom is always captivated by this part of the process and often goes, "Awww."

Once every hair is in its proper place, I can rest easy and wait for Mom or the man to stroll by and admire me. Alternatively, I'm now prepared to use my adorableness to persuade others to do my bidding.

I saunter into the next room, feeling confident and stylish. Mom is hunched over her laptop at the kitchen table, gazing intently at the bright screen. I decide that she should pause this activity and adore me.

I surprise her by bounding onto the table and nudging her hand with my nose. She stops tapping the black squares and looks up at me. I lift my ears, give her a wide-eyed stare, and tilt my head slightly for maximum effect. Her face softens, and she breaks into a warm smile. My powers are working nicely, and she seems to have forgotten what she was doing.

Mom strokes my cheek and coos softly. I'm certain that she is admiring my strong jaw and perfectly spaced whiskers. When she pauses, I emit a small meow, which encourages her to pet the other cheek. We lean forward and softly touch our noses. I take a moment to inhale her scent and carefully inspect her face while I'm in such close proximity. She responds with a happy sound, and my heart soars. I press my head to hers and gently rub it against her cheek, totally unconcerned about ruining the fur style that I worked so hard to perfect. She returns the nuzzle, and I purr faintly.

Mom leans back in her chair, and I drop onto her lap. She wraps her arms around me in a loving embrace, and I sit quietly for a few minutes, enjoying the warmth and security. It's so peaceful, and I can hear her heart beating. I rest my head against her chest, and she pets my back in a soothing rhythm while speaking tenderly.

I crane my neck to get a better look when a disturbance down the hall interrupts our peaceful moment. The man is shuffling around in the bathroom, where water falls from the ceiling into the large white tub. My curiosity takes over, and after one last nuzzle, I hop down to investigate.

I tiptoe silently over to the open doorway and watch his movements with interest. He picks up the blue toothbrush and slathers the end with white goo from a tube. Using the bristles, he spreads the substance across his teeth, getting it into every nook and cranny. The goo smells strange and artificial, and I want to plug my nose. Why would he eat that stuff? A moment later, he spits it out, which is exactly what I would do.

The man turns a small silver handle, and water gushes out of a hooked spout into the sink. He applies another type of goo to his face and massages it onto his skin, forming a frothy coating. Then, to my horror, the man repeatedly splashes water onto his face to remove the foam. I cringe just watching the slippery droplets fall from his chin.

Humans seem to enjoy playing in the water, and this makes no sense to me. I would never voluntarily get my face wet. If there was even a chance I would be drenched, I would sprint away in the opposite direction and hide until the coast was clear.

The man doesn't share my anxiety and simply wipes his face with a towel and goes on with his grooming routine as though nothing was amiss. He runs his fingers through his hair, much like I do, and then does something truly alarming. From two small containers, he produces clear, round lenses that he gently presses onto his eyes. I can't stand to watch this part. He blinks a few times and seems unconcerned at having foreign objects in his eyes.

I wonder if he's part alien or a robot that has to replace its eye coverings periodically. He appears to be human, but it could be a skillful ruse. I've been observing him for months now, waiting to see if he replaces any other parts that break down. I don't have much evidence so far, but I'll be watching.

Assuming he is human, I've tried to show him and Mom my preferred grooming routine. It doesn't involve any water, can be done anywhere, and helps improve flexibility. Actually, it's really a form of yoga combined with personal hygiene, which makes it a very efficient option for those of us with impossibly busy schedules. Despite demonstrating my system multiple times, they haven't shown interest in adopting it and appear content to use the unsettling water method.

I lose interest in watching the man and shudder at the thought of any stray droplets splattering me. I wander back to the bedroom to make sure the snuggle time with Mom didn't mess up my hair. I'll need to ramp up my cuteness so I can secure an early dinner tonight.

Quest for Greatness

I consider myself to be a brave explorer and a great scientist. In my many years, I've scouted several territories and meticulously mapped their rooms, making note of the tall vantage points, soft nap areas, water sources, and food storage zones. I keep a detailed inventory of the useful resources and note any potential threats in the region. I like to be well informed and prepared for any scenario.

In my prior home, there were six rooms, eight lookout points, five water sources, and two food storage locations. We kept a large sack of dry kibble, a bag of treats, and at least ten cans of wet food in stock at all times. It was a well-supplied stronghold with many topographical merits.

The only threats were the gray-winged fiends, commonly known as pigeons, that would fly in from above, land in a flutter on the window ledge, and stare into my home with their beady eyes. They

71

would strut along, bob their heads, and coo menacingly. At times, there would be only one scout, but they often traveled in packs.

I made it my mission to carefully study these creatures and determine their weaknesses so that if one ever broke through the glass barriers protecting my residence, it could be easily neutralized. I would stalk them when they perched on the ledges and watch them flit about, spying through one window and then another. They seemed intent on invading the privacy of my inner sanctum and finding an access point for their imminent invasion.

In my current home, there are five rooms, ten high ledges, five water sources, and one food stockpile location. There is a bag of kibble, two containers of treats, and fifteen cans of wet food in our supply depot. Ideally, we should diversify our food storage in case thieves attempt to raid our resources. I'll have to organize a cargo transport to move an emergency stash into another room. It's always smart to have a backup plan.

While conducting my weekly inspection of the food stores, I notice a slight movement in the window. I pause and hone in on the area, my eyes growing wide with interest. Everything is still for a moment, and then I see something wriggling along the ledge outside.

Life by Pumpkin: A Cat's Tale

I invoke my stealth mode and steal closer, hoping it doesn't spot me and run away before I can conduct a thorough analysis. I leap onto my climbing tower and press my belly to the soft surface, trying to elude detection for as long as possible.

On the other side of the window, clinging to the mesh screen that lets air in but keeps me from breaking out, is a small green critter. It has an oblong body, a slender tail, and needle-like claws that allow it to hang from the mesh. I have not encountered this particular species before, but I believe it's a member of the lizard family.

A few minutes pass, and it neither retreats to safety nor acknowledges my presence. I inch forward for a closer look, pausing frequently and pretending not to be interested. I don't want to spook this thing before documenting it for my studies. From this angle, I can see that it's covered in small shiny scales that fade from light green on its underside to dark green on its back. It doesn't resemble fur at all. No one would want to cuddle this critter, as it does not possess my cuteness powers.

I creep closer, and as I approach, it crawls halfway up the screen, freezes, and looks down at me, tilting its head one way and then the other. Those beady eyes lock onto mine, and we engage in an intense staring contest. I'm determined not to look away, but the urge to blink builds as the seconds tick by. The silence is heavy, and I can tell that the creature is deciding whether to fight or flee. I take another step forward, and it scampers further up the mesh, breaking eye contact. I win!

The front door opens, and I whirl around to see who has arrived and disturbed my studies. Mom shoves a large box into the house, using her foot to push it across the floor so the door can swing closed. This is an interesting development.

I lose interest in the mesh clinger and hop down from the ledge. That's enough research for one day. Mom is busy opening the box and unloading its bounty. I investigate the contents, but it's useless stuff that I didn't order. This must have come from the magic delivery network that Mom can access. After she somehow sends a message out to the universe, a bag or box containing the desired item is delivered. One of the network servants brings it right to our door and then scurries away. If I only knew how it worked, I could have all the wet food in the region delivered before dinner. My stomach rumbles just thinking about it.

While I have no use for the items that arrived in our shipment today, the box itself looks promising. It's large, with tall sides that I have to leap over to gain entry. This kind of fortification will provide solid protection from any approaching enemies. I could hunker down in the box and wait them out while they attempt to breach the high walls.

Once the box is empty, I catapult myself through the air, crashing through the flaps on top and landing gracefully within. I duck under one of the crushed panels, and it springs back into place above my head, concealing me completely. This makes for an excellent hiding spot, and I press my face against the small crack between the flaps to stare out. This lookout spot will allow me to spy on anyone in the vicinity and learn their secrets.

The box is spacious, and I appreciate the darkness created by the flimsy panels overhead. This is the perfect vessel to transport me to unexplored territories that may contain valuable resources. My mind begins to wander as I consider the possibilities. Perhaps Mousey can install wings on this thing, and we can fly like those birds we see flitting from branch to branch in the tree just beyond the window. This would be a highly efficient mode of transportation and is far superior to walking from place to place. Those noisy little creatures make it look easy, but so far, I've been unable to master that skill. It's possible that my furry paws just aren't designed for flight, but I'm not willing to admit failure yet.

My head bumps against one of the flaps, and I pause for a moment before nudging it again. The panel lifts up and flutters back down with a soft noise. Excitement bubbles up within me as I realize that this box is equipped with its own set of wings. If I can unfold them, then I believe this transport vehicle will loosely resemble the chirpy birds that I've been observing. Quickly, I burst through the panels, knocking them open and causing them to fold toward the outside of the box, where they hang suspended, bobbing slightly from the impact. I check both sides and am pleased that they are a similar shape to the birds' wings and can hinge up and down. I tap one paw against a flap, watching it droop with the added weight and spring back when I pull away. Excellent! I think this contraption is indeed flightworthy.

"Mousey! Ready a crew, we're going on an adventure!" I call, looking around for a start button and a steering mechanism.

There's no apparent control panel, which poses a real mechanical challenge. I suppose we could try changing course by shifting our weight from side to side, but this seems like a rudimentary method, and this sophisticated piece of equipment must have a high-tech solution.

I pace back and forth in the small space, contemplating the issue. I paw at the walls in case there's some kind of pressure-sensitive panel hidden in plain sight. Everything seems solid, and I sit quietly to consider other options.

Then the obvious solution presents itself. This device must be equipped with mind-reading technology that will allow me to direct it with a mere thought. It has likely already established a connection to my brain and is waiting patiently for direction. Satisfied that I have resolved this major flight impediment, I scoot forward to what I assume is the front of the vehicle.

"Mousey, what is taking so long? Bring some snacks, my water bowl, the fluffy blanket, and a few of my troops, and then we can be on our way," I cry, feeling impatient and slightly annoyed at having to ask a second time.

I conduct one last safety check as an added precaution. The wings appear to be in working order, and I tap one again for good measure. It rebounds and settles back into its former position, exactly as expected. The walls are solid, with no evident cracks or weaknesses. The transport is clear of all obstacles in the area, and I think we're ready for liftoff.

The mouse forces have yet to respond, and my frustration is mounting. They seem to follow orders when they are within swatting distance, but once I'm out of sight, they get lazy. I often catch them lounging on the floor when I've clearly been calling their names. This behavior shows a complete disregard for my authority, and I'll not stand for insubordination. I'll have to punish them upon my return from this exploratory mission. They may also be cowards and too afraid of the great unknown to accompany me. This thought makes me feel incredibly superior, and I take a moment to revel in it.

"This is Transport One warning all surrounding vehicles of my imminent liftoff. Clear the airspace and keep a safe distance to avoid collisions," I announce, wondering how many other boxes might be floating around. "Again, Transport One is ready for takeoff. Clear the area."

I take a calming breath and try to focus my energy on the mental connection to the vehicle. I envision the flaps beginning to wave up and down, gently lifting the box into the air, where it will hover a few inches above the floor. I think it's best to take this slow and get a feel for the steering system before blasting off to parts unknown. The vehicle doesn't respond to my command, and I peer over the side to confirm that it's still solidly on the floor. Hiccups are to be expected when performing any new activity, and I'm sure there is a learning curve. I again focus on communicating with the transport and can picture it floating effortlessly into the air. I close my eyes, just in case that helps with the connection. Seconds tick by, and I don't sense any movement. My eyes fly open, and I glance around, disappointed to find that the box is still firmly on the floor.

Life by Pumpkin: A Cat's Tale

This thing must be broken. It isn't responding to any of my instructions, and there must be a damaged circuit somewhere. We're going to have to open up the walls and troubleshoot the issue. I'll admit that I'm not well versed in the mechanics of this contraption, but no matter—how hard can it be? I suppose this adventure will have to be delayed until tomorrow while we make the necessary repairs.

"Mousey, bring the toolbox and Ball of Yarn. We're going to figure this out together," I command, hoping he'll respond now that the potentially dangerous mission is on hold.

While this malfunction is a temporary setback, I remain immensely pleased with the acquisition of such a cutting-edge vehicle. Once it is operational, I'll resume my quest for world dominance—I mean, exploration.

No Doors Shall Be Closed

It's a beautiful sunny afternoon, and I've been lounging on the bed, watching Mom dutifully organize my home. She's a diligent worker, and I appreciate her meticulous approach to housekeeping. My interior design preferences could be described as elegant with a hint of superiority, but it all starts with cleanliness. In my opinion, décor can hardly be considered elegant if it's dirty.

Mom is an essential part of my design and maintenance team, although she doesn't take direction well. We're working on her communication skills because she doesn't understand feline. You would think that after all these years, she would've developed a rudimentary understanding of the language, but alas, she struggles in this department. We have established a system of facial expressions, meaningful looks, meows, purrs, and other body language cues that generally do the trick. It's mainly about her understanding and responding to me, not the other way around. I do what I want.

Anyway, Mom began cleaning up this morning without any encouragement. She has come to understand my preferences and is taking the initiative to carry out my wishes. I no longer have to assign chores because she's so well-trained and completes them on her own.

I like to monitor her proceedings to ensure that everything is done to my high standards. In any situation, I believe you get the best results by being present and overseeing the task. This helps with accountability so Mom doesn't start slacking off on the job.

She's currently scrubbing the floors, and I watch with mild interest as she drags around a long stick with a white pad attached to the bottom. It sprays out a floral-smelling liquid and is then used to mop the area, dispersing the liquid in the general vicinity. This process leaves the floor shiny and clean, but the scent lingers, and I find it a bit overpowering. I make a note to request odorless cleaning supplies for the next round of chores. Mom systematically moves around the room and is incredibly thorough, most likely because I'm closely monitoring her progress.

After cleaning the floor, she begins wiping down surfaces with a fresh towel. She first removes all loose items from the furniture before spraying it with more pungent liquid and scrubbing it with a cloth to make it shine and appear brand new. I flick one ear nervously as she moves toward the nightstand that holds my water cup because I despise when people disturb my possessions.

She places my cup on the floor, and I wince since the ground is dirty, and for cleanliness reasons, the cup should never be placed there. Although the floor has recently been sanitized, I continue to object to this practice and will have to insist that she simply transfer it to the other nightstand in the future. I try not to focus on the cup and instead stare out the window until this chore is completed.

I climb to my feet and rush over to inspect the damage. The cup is almost perfectly aligned on the small stone coaster, the purpose of which I don't fully understand. Maybe it raises the cup to my preferred drinking height, which I appreciate. I take a tiny sip and use my nose to gently nudge the cup back into position. All is well again, and I sigh in relief.

Mom has moved on to the next room, so I step to the end of the bed and keep an eye on her. It's a warm day, so the internal temperature control system activates. One of the wall vents blows directly on me from my vantage point, and I enjoy the cool breeze. I scoot over to bask in the artificial wind, raise my head high, and close my eyes. I take long, relaxing breaths and try to quiet my racing thoughts. For a brief period, the world is silent, and I slip into a peaceful state of mind. As I relax, my mouth drops open, revealing my pink tongue. My long whiskers flutter gently as the chilly air caresses them. It tickles a little, but it's also a soothing feeling. This continues for a few minutes before the mechanical temperature system shuts down, and the air is still again.

I open my eyes after the blissful moment, feeling rejuvenated and energized. I shake my head, unsure what to do next. Mom is making a lot of noise as she continues with her chores and disappears into the bathroom. In violation of my rules and regulations, she closes the door behind her. I've mandated that all doors remain open in this house so I may come and go at my leisure. Mom is aware of this rule but often forgets and has to be reminded.

I hop down and stroll across the now-sanitary floor. Approaching the closed door, I let out a soft meow and wait for Mom to respond. She's definitely in there but doesn't immediately answer my request for entry.

"Hey, remember what I said about closing doors? Open this at once, and let me in!" I yell. "I don't like to be kept waiting."

I rise up onto my back paws and pound my front paws against the door a few times, meowing simultaneously. I hear movement, and the door cracks open, allowing me to squeeze inside. Mom shoves it closed again, and I survey the situation. She is seated on the human equivalent of my sandbox, which is basically a white bowl full of water. I always wonder why she doesn't use a normal sandbox.

To give her some privacy, I turn my back and stare at the closed door. My sandbox has a cover, so no one can see what I'm doing in there. I feel that she deserves the same courtesy, although this room is much larger, and my presence is minimally invasive.

A moment later, I hear the sound of rushing water. This step of the process always makes me uneasy because I despise uncontrolled water. Mom then walks over to the sink, where water falls into a sunken cavity and flows down a black hole. She runs her hands under the water and dries them on a hanging towel. I don't know what this accomplishes, and I'm disturbed that she voluntarily gets wet and then wipes the water on a perfectly comfy-looking towel that could serve as additional bedding if it were dry and on the ground.

Alas, I know there are human habits that I'll never understand, and I try to accept them and not judge my humans too harshly. Okay, I do judge Mom for this, but I keep that to myself.

Mom opens the small door beneath the sink, places something inside the cabinet, and closes it with a thud. She then strides out of the room to resume her cleaning duties. There are still a few hours remaining in her shift, and I'm delighted with her enthusiasm.

In her absence, I turn my full attention to the compartment. I'm curious about its contents and take issue with this door being closed. I paw at the little, polished handle in an effort to gain a firm grip. Because of my silky fur, it only opens an inch before I lose contact, and it slams shut again. I repeat this process, first with one paw and then with the other. My efforts are rewarded with thud sounds that grow louder and more frequent as my technique improves.

Mom peers into the room and observes my activities. I raise my head and give her a look that says, "There's nothing to see here."

She usually tells me to stop doing stuff like this, but I never listen. I generally try to stay hidden and avoid detection so I can snoop at my leisure. To my surprise, Mom slowly opens the cabinet door and does not deter me from entering. I watch her for a moment, trying to determine her motives. Curiosity wins, and I peek into the tiny space.

It's crammed with bottles and rolls of soft paper. I turn my nose up at the stench of the containers, which smell like the cleaning solutions Mom has been using. There isn't much of interest here, but there's a sliver of unoccupied space in the back that

I want to search for hidden treasure. I tread carefully around the bottles, knocking one or two of them over in the process. They roll out of the cabinet and across the floor, but Mom can pick them up later. There's limited room to move around, but the empty space toward the back has just enough square footage for me to sit down.

I look around, taking a quick inventory of the supplies that Mom is stockpiling. This is an excellent hiding space if I can solve the polished handle issue. Growing bored of the confined space, I amble out, knocking a few more bottles over along the way. I wander between Mom's legs, softly rubbing against her as a thank you for her hard work and assistance in accessing the secret compartment. Then I retire to my bedroom for an afternoon nap, confident that she'll complete the remaining chores without my supervision. My work is finished here.

Training the Beasts

I've become accustomed to the constant presence of the man's two fluffy dogs. I would prefer to greet them as occasional visitors and not as permanent guests who lounge around on the floor and scatter fur about with reckless disregard for my cleanliness standards, but I know they're here to stay.

They're big and awkward at times, so I give them a wide berth when they get excited and start prancing around. They make no attempt to control their emotions, which I believe is a tactical mistake. I only express love and adoration for humans when they've done something that pleases me and is worth rewarding with my affection. If I expressed joy over simply being in their presence, then they wouldn't put in the required effort to gain my attention, and I wouldn't be able to easily manipulate them. This thought makes me feel far superior to my golden-haired comrades.

Careful observation and experimentation have revealed that these two companions are fairly trainable and generally bow down to my wishes. These are very desirable traits for my subjects and are the dogs' best qualities by far.

We recently relocated to a new estate, and I'm working on establishing boundaries and protocols. The beasts have just returned from one of their brief adventures outside and are clearly excited. I observe them from my perch on the kitchen table and consider which training guide would be most helpful in this situation.

When the dogs settle down, I drop to the ground and swagger over, exuding utter confidence and supremacy. I take a seat next to the couch, and they give me a wary look. This is a good start. They already regard me as a force to be reckoned with. I remain silent for a few moments, staring at them intently and allowing the tension to build.

"Listen up. You may freely roam the area from the edge of the couch to the front door, but you will not cross this line," I declare, pacing the distance between the couch and the wall. "Mom's desk, where she sits with the laptop contraption and taps away, is also part of my territory, and I reserve the right to pass through your designated area to reach it."

They don't respond and glance about with blank expressions. We sometimes have communication issues because they don't speak feline, and I have no desire to learn their language.

"Do you understand?" I inquire, trying to be patient.

They just stare at me, and the large one with the limp suddenly lies down, lifts her leg, and begins to lick her rear. Feeling embarrassed and uneasy, I look away and wait for her to finish. When I have her attention again, I outline the boundaries by pacing the space beside the couch, wandering over to Mom's desk, and hopping atop it to glare down at them.

This is not the first time I've schooled the beasts about boundaries, and they normally follow my instructions. However, I'm a firm believer in the need for repetition in training and reiterate this lesson at least once a week. I don't want them to develop a false sense of security and begin walking around aimlessly. When that happens, I have to herd them back into their designated space and stand guard for a while to ensure they stay put.

I believe my allocation of space is very generous, and I'm proud to be such a benevolent ruler. They may freely roam the entry room from the front door to the couch, except for the desk area, of course, and I have claims on the remainder of the house. They appear to enjoy snoozing near the door while waiting for Mom to come home, and they sleep on the couch at night. To be honest, they have everything they need in this designated area, and I'm not sure what else they could want.

Allowing them this room is also strategic from a home security perspective, as it places them close to the door. They are the first line of defense should an intruder attempt to breach our borders. If that happens, I'll finally see what these two are capable of, although hopefully it never comes to that.

The one that hobbles suddenly scrambles to her feet and approaches my position. I stand my ground and look her in the eyes. She stops about a foot away and raises her head to gaze at me with an innocent expression on her shaggy face. Neither of us moves, and she casts a glance behind her at the nervous one, who, as usual, appears slightly terrified. I display my agitation by rotating one ear sideways and flicking my tail rhythmically. The fur on my back begins to stand on end, but I attempt to keep my cool. She approaches and tilts her head upward as though to sniff my feet.

In a flash, I raise one paw and whack her on the nose, causing her to step back. The dog's eyes are wide with confusion, and she appears shocked by the swift rebuff. She stares at me for a long time, then looks down at the floor, then back at me. Her mouth falls open, and she begins to pant softly. I'm concerned because I've seen her lick Mom and the man with her long, slobbery tongue.

She approaches the desk again after a few tense moments, licking her nose in the process. She raises her head and is now too close for comfort with that dripping tongue. Sensing danger, I reach out and angle her nose down with one paw, directing the foul-smelling breath toward the floor and preventing any attempt to lick me. That's disgusting, and I'm not going to put up with this behavior.

She retreats again, clearly puzzled and trying to make sense of what's happening. These beasts are not the brightest, and I try to be patient during training sessions. I'm sure they want to please me, but it's initially difficult for them to grasp my instructions.

She stretches her neck toward me for a third time but then pauses, and we exchange a knowing look before she lies down with her head upon her paws. Success! I feel a sense of pride and perch on the edge of the desk, head raised high, savoring the moment. Despite the size of these beasts, I have tamed them thanks to my superior intelligence.

The skittish dog has been observing these proceedings and hopefully learning something. She looks nervous and tries to sneak a few brief glances at me before turning to stare at her companion and then at the floor. She lies down and rests her head on her paws, expelling a deep sigh.

Satisfied that my work here is done, I hop to the ground and amble away to take a quick nap. I flop down on the floor to enjoy the heat as the afternoon sun streams through the windows. Teaching is a physically demanding job, and I need to regain my strength for the next session.

I wake up thirty minutes later, feeling rejuvenated and relaxed. Climbing to my feet, I arch my back and stretch my front paws out as far as they can go. This helps loosen up tight muscles after lying in one spot for so long. I yawn lazily and shake my head, attempting to cast off the remnants of sleep.

Now, what should I do with my afternoon? My calendar is completely free, and there are so many possibilities. I could sit in the window and monitor my kingdom, take an inventory of my food reserves, conduct training exercises with my mouse army, or take another nap and evaluate the options again later.

As I'm contemplating the situation, I catch sight of Bow under the table. She has been quiet today, and I wonder if she's bored and wants to run around. I approach slowly, and she remains motionless. I reach out and nudge her gently, and she leaps into action, skittering a few feet away before pausing. The game has begun! I chase her down and give her a stronger shove, sending her spinning across the wood floor with a delightful scratching sound. I'm close on her heels and swat her again before she comes to a complete stop.

We've been working on her aim because she has had trouble staying on course, and this time she careens toward the shaggy dog resting beneath the desk. The dog lifts her head and contemplates Bow as she slides to a halt a foot away. I watch in horror as the beast scoots forward for a lengthy sniff, hoping she won't devour Bow.

I race over to diffuse this delicate situation. The dog looks at me warily, but her silly, cheerful demeanor quickly returns. Bow remains silent, and I feel horrible that she has to put up with that stinky panting. How could I be so careless as to chase a valued friend into the dogs' designated area? I had previously outlined the boundaries, and now I've inadvertently crossed them.

"Bow and the rest of my toys are completely off-limits to you," I state emphatically. "Don't even think about touching her."

When the dog leans forward again, I leap into action. I advance in a zigzag fashion, snatching Bow in my teeth. This aggressive behavior startles the dog, who awkwardly gets to her feet and lopes away to the other side of the room. I'm greatly pleased by this response.

"Look here," I say, gently placing Bow at my feet. "I am reclaiming this space and redrawing the boundary here. If you cross this line, I will have no choice but to retaliate. My decision is final, and I will not take any questions at this time."

The dogs just stare at me, so I carry Bow over to the kitchen table and carefully place her on the ground. Despite the close call, she appears unfazed, and I'm relieved that she wasn't injured by those brutes.

I return to the sunny patch on the floor and lie down for a short rest. That's enough excitement for one day.

Competing for Affection

Mom is wedged between the golden-haired dogs on the couch and is petting them affectionately while whispering softly. The skittish one is curled up with her head resting on Mom's lap. She appears content and at ease, lulled into a meditative state by the soothing caresses. I absolutely understand the feeling, as one of my favorite pastimes is lounging on Mom's lap while she showers me with love and affection. This whole situation irritates me.

The shaggy dog with the bad leg is standing beside Mom and occasionally licks her arm. She looks longingly at Mom's lap, but there isn't enough room for her to crawl onto it. The dogs are far too large and ungainly to be held the way Mom cradles me.

As I watch this touching scene, I begin to feel unsettled. The beasts are monopolizing Mom's time and copying my signature moves to solicit attention. I can't permit this behavior to continue and must put a stop to it at once. I'm the only one who should be allowed on Mom's lap, and the dogs have no right to occupy that exclusive spot without my permission. I'm not jealous; I'm just possessive.

Mom pauses to check her phone, and the skittish dog paws at her until she resumes scratching her back. The beast calms down and her peaceful expression returns. Now I'm concerned that Mom is being forced to pet them at the risk of being relentlessly pawed at or worse. This will not be tolerated in my home.

I formulate a plan while pacing back and forth, the tension increasing with every passing second. I need to gain Mom's attention first, so I hop up onto the low table in front of the couch, where she can't possibly ignore me. She smiles at my approach and says something warmly. This is a good sign, and now I just need to lead her to safety. I move to the front of the table and give the beasts a skeptical look.

Mom extends her hand, and I rub warmly against her, delighted to be the center of attention. She scratches the itchy spots behind my ears, and I begin to purr involuntarily. Mom knows exactly how I like my massages.

She then pauses and resumes petting the beasts. This annoys me, and I walk from one side of the table to the other. She doesn't look at me, so I let out a soft meow that forces her to refocus on me. I hold her gaze, my eyes wide and my head tilted slightly for maximum cuteness. It's time to employ my superpowers to persuade her to do as I say.

She reaches out and rubs my cheeks and chin once more. I close my eyes, raise my head, and sink into her embrace. The sound of the dogs' collars jingling jolts me from my stupor, and I open my eyes to find the shaggy one staring at me. She's a bit too close for comfort, and I consider giving her a little swat on the nose to regain some personal space. However, she seems satisfied with simply observing and makes no move to further encroach or to lick me, which would be a disgusting breach of my rules. If she ever licks me, it will do irreparable harm to our relationship. I don't know how I could forgive her for that kind of uninvited intimacy.

The skittish one is pawing at Mom again, who obliges her request for a belly rub. The dog rolls onto her back, all four legs awkwardly sticking up in the air. This is something I would never do because I'm aware of the dangers of exposing my delicate underbelly. I consider pouncing on her in this vulnerable position, but our size disparity makes me hesitate. I may be faster and smarter, but the dogs are considerably stronger, and I don't want to take my chances in a physical altercation.

Leslie Popp

I make an effort to conceal my irritation at having to compete for Mom's attention and stare out the window to collect my thoughts before making any rash moves. I have an understanding with the dogs, and they are learning to obey my wishes. They have been responding reasonably well to consistent training, and perhaps this is just another situation that needs to be addressed in my next lesson plan. They must be reminded that I was here first and have dibs on Mom's time and attention. The dogs are only allowed to spend this kind of quality time with her if I'm otherwise occupied. We'll start working on this at their next session. In the interim, I will have to schedule a time to speak with Ms. Fish to vent my frustration. She's a great listener who never questions my opinions and is always sympathetic to my challenges. She doesn't say much, but we're close, and I understand what she's thinking.

I return my attention to the disturbing situation at hand. The shaggy dog with the limp is once again completely focused on Mom and is happily leaning against her leg while Mom rubs her back. My fur bristles, and my annoyance grows with every second that I'm not the center of attention.

I'm drawn to the dog's long golden tail, which is wagging vigorously back and forth. The movement reminds me of something, and I can't take my eyes off it. It swings wildly, bumping repeatedly into the side of the table, nearly sweeping all of the items resting atop it to the ground.

I crouch down into a pounce position and take a step toward the beast. She has her back to me and seems unaware of her surroundings. The predator in me awakens and instinct takes hold. A primal feeling washes over me, and I'm captivated by the thrill of the hunt.

I advance, keeping my belly pressed against the table as I creep silently toward the dog. When I reach the edge, I pause and stare intently as her tail sways back and forth, mocking me. I raise my front paw and wait for the perfect moment, trying to time the trajectory. Seizing the opportunity, I lash out and swat her tail as it arcs toward me. She looks over her shoulder in surprise, but the blow seems to have little effect. Her tail continues to wag as though nothing happened.

I view this as an invitation and prepare to take another swing. For a moment, I just watch, swaying with the rhythm. On the second pass, I strike, connecting solidly with my target. A few pieces of fur become caught in my claws, and I'm left staring at the long strands dangling from my paw.

When the dog turns to face me, I realize it's time to retreat and regroup. I trot to the other side of the room and bound onto my climbing tower before she can retaliate. I'm now firmly in my territory, and she wouldn't dare follow me over here.

Moments later, Mom comes looking for me, possibly concerned that I was feeling excluded and neglected, which I was. She approaches, rests her hand on my cheek, and plants a tender kiss on the top of my head. I softly purr as my heart soars, feeling immensely satisfied and proud of myself. She gently rubs my back, finally giving me her full attention. I close my eyes as the soothing touch lulls me into a meditative state. The purring grows louder, and I drop my head onto my paws as I drift off into an afternoon nap.

While I may have to remind the beasts who the favorite is around here, I'll always be Mom's special boy. She loves me unconditionally, and no dog could ever come between us. What would I do without her?

Mini-Me

They say imitation is the sincerest form of flattery. I don't know who they are, but I know someone said it, and truer words were never spoken. As a handsome, smart, and beloved tabby cat, I find that others are often jealous of my luxurious lifestyle. It makes sense that everyone would like to be me. Who wouldn't?

I worked hard to build a wonderful life for myself. It started with selecting the right human and forever home, and to this day, that remains my greatest triumph. I immediately assigned Mom the responsibility for my care and well-being, and she now faithfully handles all of my needs, so I can kick back, unwind, and enjoy my days.

My mornings start whenever I'm good and ready. If I wake up feeling drowsy, I roll over, close my eyes, and go right back to sleep. When I'm ready for breakfast, I place my order with Mom, and she dutifully prepares a delicious meal that's served in my shallow dish, which is the ideal size and depth for me to eat from without getting my whiskers dirty. Mom is aware that I only eat chicken, turkey, duck, and fish, and that I dislike combining flavors. My food must be puréed into a fine consistency because I also dislike chewing, which is a hassle.

If I'm feeling thirsty, I simply hop into the white tub in the bathroom and meow for Mom to pour cups of water in front of me until I'm ready for a cool drink. Sometimes, I just watch the liquid run into the black hole at one end of the tub, and I'll only start drinking when I'm sure it is pure and at the correct temperature.

I have an abundance of toys and loyal servants who are always eager to play with me. Mousey, Ms. Fish, Bow, and Ball of Yarn enjoy lying on the ground and patiently waiting for playtime. My visits are undoubtedly the highlight of their day, as their other activities appear to be somewhat dull.

When I require attention, I simply insert myself into whatever activity Mom is engaged in and persuade her to stop and pet me. She generally obeys and gives me the time and attention I deserve. She's always busy, and I wish she had more free time to focus on me and my needs.

Mom gifted me our current residence, which has several rooms and many towering surfaces to perch atop. I have free reign of the place, which is equipped with two soft beds and a marvelous climbing tower. The views are wonderful, and I enjoy gazing out the window to observe my other subjects going about their day. I haven't met many of them, but as the ruler of this realm, I'm quite busy and want my subordinates to remember that my time is precious.

I'm wandering through my many rooms, considering how envious others must be, when I realize that the door to the bedroom's spacious wardrobe is ajar. It has been a while since I explored the depths of these shelves. I nudge the door open further and assess the contents.

There are several low shelves piled high with the many human furs that Mom and the man slip on and off each day. I don't understand these odd coverings that come in a variety of shapes, colors, and textures. Mom doesn't have natural fur, except on the top of her head. Perhaps she needs these substitute furs to keep her warm because she doesn't possess her own fluffy coat.

I wonder what all of the human furs might be concealing. The shelves are full, and they would be the perfect hiding place for something important and enticing. This would also be an excellent place to nap because I would be off the ground and hidden from prying eyes. Sometimes, I just need alone time to unwind.

One by one, I remove the stack of human furs on the bottom shelf and set them on the floor. They topple over in a messy pile, but Mom can sort that out later. The second and third stacks soon follow, leaving the shelf completely bare. To my dismay, there are no hidden treasures behind the human furs, and I'm left staring at the empty shelf. I crawl into the small space, test it for napping purposes, and decide that it will do nicely. I rest a while, enjoying the fruits of my labor. Looking out at the mess of discarded human furs, I decide that the assortment on the floor would also make a cozy bed. So many options, and only four naps a day.

I realize that the absence of a secret stash on the first shelf doesn't mean that there isn't something of interest on the second one. I drop down to the floor, stretch to my full height, and begin removing items from the next shelf. They rain down around me, and it looks like a small hurricane swept through the room. I hop onto the second empty shelf and scoot to the back to check for hidden panels that might contain something of value. This shelf also proves to be completely ordinary and uninteresting. Perhaps Mom is more creative with her hiding spots than I originally thought.

I hop back down to the ground and am about to begin working on the third shelf when I hear the front door open and note Mom's footsteps heading this way. Looking around at the disarray, I scour my brain for a simple explanation that doesn't implicate me. Mom enters the room as I'm fleeing the crime scene and tosses the outer covering, which she wears outside over her human fur, onto the bed. I try to distract her from the disheveled state of the room.

She pauses and stares at the human furs strewn haphazardly on the floor. I refuse to look in that direction, and when her gaze settles on me, I turn away and pretend that the plain white wall has piqued my interest.

"I've never noticed how flat and white this wall is before," I think to myself. "Now that I take a closer look, I realize it's not white at all; it's off-white."

Mom sighs, whispers my name, and sets to work repairing the damage I've caused. I step onto her outer covering, which is still warm from her body heat, as she reorganizes the wardrobe. I curl up and wrap my tail around myself, enjoying the cozy feel and her lingering scent. This is an excellent heating blanket, and I could use one of these before every nap.

Mom returns to collect her outer covering after cleaning up my mess and pauses when she notices me happily bedded down. I look up at her with wide, innocent eyes, trying to convince her that I would never dream of sifting through her belongings while she was away. I have the utmost respect for other people's privacy, so it must have been one of the dogs.

Mom doesn't seem too bothered by the situation, which I take as yet another sign of her unwavering love. It's as though I can do no wrong. I certainly adopted the right human.

Mom wanders away but returns a moment later with one hand behind her back. I wonder what surprise she has in store for me today. I hope it's a new recruit for my mouse army or a fresh bag of chicken treats with soft centers and crunchy exteriors. They are my favorite and come in a cheery yellow bag that makes a distinct crinkling sound when opened. It acts as an alarm, alerting me to stop what I'm doing and rush over to devour the savory morsels.

Mom rubs my back a few times and presses her forehead against mine. In return for her loyal service and affection, I gently touch my nose to hers. Mom then presents me with a perplexing object—a fluffy cat-shaped creature. She places it beside me, and I roll over to carefully inspect this intriguing present. It has long whiskers, orange stripes, a patch of white on its face, and big black eyes. A long sniff reveals that it's definitely not alive and may have more in common with Ms. Fish or Mousey. It's far too large to be one of my toys and closely resembles my own stature. Our fur colors and patterns are similar, although my stripes are not marred by white spots on my face and paws. I reach out to touch it and find that it's soft, squishes easily, and lacks bone structure.

It appears that an artist created a sculpture in my honor to celebrate my silky fur, elegant whiskers, and handsome face. This creature bears a vague resemblance to me, although I'm far more handsome and regal in appearance. It's a bit crude and must have been made by an amateur. Still, I'm honored by the offering and shall display it somewhere prominent for all to see. Perhaps this will inspire others to present me with comparable gifts, and over time, I will create a gallery full of my own likenesses. All great leaders need a dedicated room to celebrate their magnificence and ensure that they are remembered throughout the ages.

The fact that complete strangers are using me as a model for their craft will do wonders to help spread my name far and wide. If these works of art can be distributed across my extensive lands, then subjects in even the most remote locations will come to know my face. This will undoubtedly inspire loyalty and deter any potential usurpers from challenging my authority.

"Please thank the artist, but send them a recent photo so they can create a more accurate replica. This is an acceptable first attempt, but I hope they can improve," I tell Mom. "Then have one of these delivered to each household in my territory so everyone will know my face and can worship me."

Mom leans down and kisses the top of my head. She kneels beside the bed, holds up her phone, and calls my name. I glance over and hear a soft click. She proceeds to run her fingers over the phone, smiling as though she has done something clever. I've seen this behavior before but don't know what it means. The clicking sound usually occurs when she's holding the phone still and elevated.

"Did you not hear me?" I ask. "Put that away and see to my request at once. I am eager to have more of these produced and distributed."

She simply pats my head and murmurs something softly before walking away. I'll check in with her later for a status update. I return my gaze to my almost twin, who is lying there with a pleasant expression on his face. I lean against him, discover that he makes a decent pillow, and drift off to sleep, content with my growing fame and recognition.

Guardians

Mom occasionally brings home a new cadet for my army of toys and loyal subjects. Today, without my permission, she assigned duties to the recent recruits. I hadn't had time to properly evaluate their skill sets and was slightly annoyed that she would go behind my back like this. I know she means well, but this is crossing the line. After all, I am the master and commander around here and can't have her undermining my authority.

A small bear with a string tied around his waist is the first recruit. While he has a cordial, welcoming demeanor, I suspect he possesses great strength and agility. Mom has tied one end of his string around the handle of the bedroom door, leaving him suspended in midair and swaying slightly as the door is opened and closed. He doesn't seem to mind, but I don't understand what purpose this serves. Being tethered to one spot is not ideal in the event of an invasion by enemy forces.

I sit back and watch him for a while before tilting my head from one side to the other. Untying him is not an option since the handle is out of my reach. Mom must have had a good reason for stationing him here; all I have to do now is figure out what it was. I pace back and forth until I decide that the best course of action is to take a long afternoon nap and revisit this issue later. The bear is certainly not going anywhere.

As I stroll by, it occurs to me that from this vantage point, he can observe the comings and goings of everyone that passes through or near this door. He serves as a sentry, ensuring that only authorized guests may enter. I never considered stationing a guard at this doorway, but thinking about it now, I would feel safer knowing someone is watching my back while I sleep.

Mom is smarter than I realized, and I feel a sense of pride because she obviously learned everything from me. It's touching to see the apprentice begin to spread her wings and use her hard-earned knowledge for my benefit. I'll have to touch noses with her later as a reward for the work she has done.

I take a seat in front of the bear, and he smiles back at me. He's not very talkative, but that's okay, I think the strong, silent type will do well in this role.

Life by Pumpkin: A Cat's Tale

I lift one paw and gently reposition him, as he's leaning to one side. He swings back and forth, and I'm drawn in by the motion. My eyes grow wide, my ears stand at attention, and my heart rate accelerates. Trying to remain calm and professional during my interaction with the new cadet, I reach out once again to stop the swaying. I unintentionally extend my claws and accidentally snag one on his soft fur. As I try to pull away, he's dragged toward me until I vigorously shake that paw, dislodging him and sending him catapulting back against the door. He bounces up and down, careening this way and that. My eyes lock on his flailing form, and instinct takes over. With incredible speed and precision, I smack him with one paw, causing him to arc wildly around to the rear of the door and collide with the hard wood before rebounding to his original position.

He's no longer my loyal subject, but merely prey dangling from a short string. The bear is now my target and my captive. If he hadn't tied himself up in such an appetizing position, we might have been able to avoid this. However, he made that decision and now has to face the consequences.

I seize him with both paws and yank him toward the floor. The string offers resistance, and I lose my grip, causing him to bounce around erratically, grazing my ear in the process. This minor act of defiance only increases my determination to subdue

111

this newcomer. I grab him before he can regroup and pin him against the door, applying my sharp teeth to the string and then to the bear. He doesn't taste very good, and I quickly spit him out.

I hear a noise behind me and am temporarily distracted. Mom is standing there, quietly watching the proceedings. I turn my attention back to the bear, who's once again dangling slightly off-center.

"I'm just becoming acquainted with the new bear sentry and welcoming him to the house," I explain.

Mom crouches down and places our other recruit on the floor in front of me. She's a white and brown owl with yellow eyes and a hooked beak. Her exterior is solid, and I wonder if she possesses natural body armor or some sort of shell. It's a fantastic defense system, which makes her a valuable addition to our ranks.

There's a small lever protruding from her back that Mom turns several times before releasing the owl and rocking back on her heels. The owl begins to strut toward me, her feet marching rhythmically. She's making an unusual whirring sound that I find a little unnerving. As she approaches, I step aside, allowing her to pass, and circle around to assess the situation. I've never seen one of my toys—I mean recruits—do anything like this. The owl has a mind of her own and has decided to march in formation as a sign of loyalty. This thought sits well with me, but the jarring sound is a concern, and it echoes through the hallway. I've never heard any creature emit such a noise, and I wonder what she's trying to communicate. The sound fades, and her feet slow their pace until the hall is silent. She stands perfectly still, and I assume that she's awaiting further marching orders.

I approach cautiously, not wanting to startle the owl. She doesn't seem bothered by my proximity, so I gently tap her on the head to ensure she hasn't dozed off. She topples onto her side with her feet sticking straight out. I wait for her to get up, but she just lies there quietly, and after a while, I lightly tap her again. She slides across the floor and doesn't attempt to stand, which is concerning.

Mom intervenes and places the owl right-side up so she's facing me again. When Mom cranks the small lever, the owl reorients herself and begins her dutiful march. Her path is straight and true, and the grating noise reverberates off the walls once more. This time, I hold my ground as she approaches my position, and it becomes a standoff to see who will step aside first. To my surprise, she doesn't change course and walks straight into my leg. The owl continues marching in place while pressing up against me, seemingly unaware that I'm far too large for her to push aside. I'm not sure what to think about this odd behavior, but it does make me question her intelligence. I lift my paw, and she topples backward, her huge eyes staring up at me. Her feet keep pace even though she's no longer standing. The noise gradually fades, and she lies there peacefully.

I wait to make sure she's finished and the noise does not resume. I move closer and thoroughly inspect her. Picking the owl up in my mouth, I try to place her upright, but she just falls over. Mom comes to my aid yet again and helps the owl regain her footing.

"Listen up, cadet. You have a very impressive march, and your first assignment is to patrol this hall and ensure that only authorized guests enter the bedroom. The bear at the door will be your new partner, and I'm confident the two of you will get along splendidly," I say matter-of-factly. "Report to your post immediately, and there will be no more lying down on the job. Do you understand?"

The owl stares straight ahead, and I assume she's practicing her stoic guard stance. I head to bed, knowing that my room is safe and secure because my night watch is in place and has its orders.

Secret Fort

I hear a noise by the front door and leap up from my nap in the sunny spot on the table. Who dares to disturb my slumber? There are no visitors or appointments on my calendar today. Who in the world would drop by unannounced? Before a social visit, I require advanced notice to ensure my fur is nicely groomed and my whiskers are spread out evenly. I always want to look my best to set a good example for my loyal subjects, which requires time and energy. You can't rush good taste.

There's a disturbance at the front door, and I scamper across the room to evaluate the situation. I approach the door with caution and hear rustling noises. Perhaps this is one of the employees from the magic delivery network that brings Mom anything she wishes for and leaves it anonymously in front of the house. There's a loud knock, and I instinctively flatten my ears and hiss menacingly. I take a few steps back, unsure of what I've gotten myself into and feeling exposed in my current position. Perhaps I should find out what this individual wants before challenging them to a duel.

I don't know if this stranger is a friend or foe, and I'm surprised at how scared I am without Mom or Mousey by my side. The dogs are napping peacefully and make no move to investigate the potential threat. They're proving to be somewhat useless as a first line of defense for my residence. Although their size and stature suggest that they would excel at this task, their general laziness is a hindrance.

"Ladies, on your feet. Go and see who requests entry to my domain," I instruct the two golden-furred beasts lounging contentedly on the couch.

They lift their heads and give me watery-eyed stares. Either they don't understand, or they're ignoring direct orders. Regardless of the reason, we'll have to work on this during the next training session.

I hear heavy footsteps receding and am relieved that the individual appears to have given up and left. Perhaps they think that no one is home because we didn't answer the door or call out to send them away when they knocked. I remain near the door in case they return and take a few breaths to calm my racing heart. Mom appears a moment later, seeming oblivious to the potential threat, and makes a beeline for the door.

"Be careful," I warn. "Someone was out there making an awful racket."

She doesn't hesitate and throws open the door as I wait in anticipation. I'm relieved to see only a few brown paper bags arranged in neat rows. Mom drags them inside, displaying her incredible strength. She carries them into the kitchen two at a time, and I follow close behind. Mom tears open the bags, and I am pleased to discover that they are filled with an assortment of food, which she unloads into the refrigerator with the tricky handle.

I poke my head into one bag and take an inventory of its contents. Everything appears to be frozen, and I wonder how you're supposed to consume items in this solid state. I prefer my food at room temperature or slightly chilled, but definitely not frozen. Perhaps they're heated before being served.

Mom folds the empty bags, and I take an interest in one that has toppled over at her feet. The inside appears dark and inviting, and I wonder if it's large enough to be used as a secret fort. I crawl inside, leaving only my tail exposed. It's a bit snug, but I manage to turn around, tuck my tail in, and position myself so I can observe everyone's activities. This fort suits me perfectly, and because it's light and portable, it can be strategically positioned around the house.

Mom continues rummaging through the bags and organizing items in the cabinets around the room. I'm delighted Mom replenished her food rations so we'll be prepared in the event of an emergency. I keep a stack of canned food on hand and need to ensure Mom is taken care of and ready to open them for me. I couldn't manage those tightly sealed lids if she wasn't here to pry them open. They have a small tab on top, but my paws can't get a firm grip, probably because of my silky fur. However, they don't pose an issue for Mom, and I consider this to be one of her most valuable skills. She also knows how much water to add to my wet food to create a soft but not runny mixture, which is exactly how I like it. I wouldn't feel comfortable doing this myself because I have an aversion to water and don't want to mess with the devices that dispense it.

I see movement at the opening of the bag and hear a scuffling noise that travels from one side to the other, pausing directly behind me. I awkwardly spin around in the confined space to face the potential threat. Something lightly touches the paper and creates a scratching sound. I watch for a moment, then lash out, smacking whatever fiend is attempting to gain entry through a nonexistent back door. The walls of my fort are a bit flimsy, and I need to reinforce them after I dispel this intruder. The scratching continues, but this time the critter climbs onto the top of my fort, causing the bag to partially cave in. Not wanting to be crushed, I lunge at my antagonist and feel my paw connect with something solid before it squirms away. This creature is quick and nearly impossible to grasp through the rippling walls. I consider wriggling out and confronting it head-on, but I want to protect my new hideout and feel secure in this dark, enclosed space. The thin walls conceal my exact position and could give me the element of surprise if I choose to dart out and pounce on this opponent.

We continue this game of cat-and-mouse for a while until the scratching approaches the entrance to the fort. I can't let this menace trap me inside and must act now before it has the upper hand. Waiting patiently for my adversary to grow bolder, I plant my back legs firmly on the floor and focus on the bright entrance ahead. When the scratching is nearly at the opening, I spring forward, paws fully extended, grasp my opponent tightly, and trap it between my teeth. I hear a little yelp and realize that I'm clutching Mom's hand with her finger wedged in my mouth. I look up, astonished. Coming to my senses, I release my grip, and she pulls away to inspect her hand for damage. Luckily, I didn't bite down too hard and only used my claws sparingly. Hopefully, I haven't injured her.

Mom examines her skin closely, and I notice several red marks appearing. Although there's no blood, my claws were not as gentle as I had intended. I gaze pitifully at the ground, unsure what to do. Mom is my favorite person, and I would never deliberately hurt her. She should've known better than to get me riled up with all of that scratching. Mom has witnessed my speed and agility on numerous occasions, and of course, I would eventually triumph over my nemesis.

If she's upset and we have a falling out, I don't know what will happen. I desperately need her to open cans of food, act as a heating blanket at night, interface with the water spigots, and lavish attention on me. Being at odds with Mom over a misunderstanding like this would be devastating, and my heart begins to sink just thinking about it.

After a moment of suspense, Mom reaches out and gently rubs her other hand against my cheek. I raise my head and gaze at her with wide, sad eyes. Leaning into her touch, I begin to nuzzle her arm to express my love and affection and to demonstrate that I never intended to cause her any harm. She plants a kiss on the top of my head, chasing away my concerns. I rub against her shins, and she offers a soothing back scratch.

Mom scoops me up and cradles me against her chest. She's warm and soft, and I adore the way she smells. I'm not a fan of having my feet off the ground for too long, but I do enjoy surveying my domain from this height. I can see everything from up here, and I think about how lucky Mom is to enjoy this view all the time. Our foreheads touch, and we share a peaceful moment before I pull away and squirm to get down.

I give Mom another loving look before wandering away to chat with Ms. Fish. I'm feeling a bit stressed about what happened and need a third party's opinion on the matter. Ms. Fish always knows what to say or not to say in these situations to put me at ease.

A New Year

Something feels different tonight. I can't put my paw on it, but Mom and the man seem very excited. They pop open a green bottle, causing it to explode with a loud bang. It launches a delightful cylindrical object across the room, which bounces off the floor and rolls to a stop next to my climbing tower. I race over to investigate, intrigued by whatever game they're playing. The object is of little interest since it is colorless and lacks feathers or fur. When shoved, it rolls nicely, and I can see this being an entertaining pastime. I'll stow it in my toy box for safekeeping because I like to be ready for anything, and it might come in handy later.

Mom and the man are sipping happily from small glasses with thin handles and wide, round bases. The liquid inside is pale yellow, with little bubbles rising up in lazy arcs. They appear to be having a good time and have been laughing and chatting all evening. Mom was busy in the kitchen this afternoon, preparing something fancy for dinner that still smelled like a combination of the plants she loves eating. This must be a special occasion, and I don't understand why they wouldn't indulge in a scrumptious meal of chicken, turkey, duck, or fish. These delicacies are never featured on their plates, which makes me slightly concerned about their health. I couldn't live without these basic foods and would reject any plants that showed up in my bowl. Plants belong in the ground, where they emerge naturally, not in my dinner dish. However, this cuisine makes Mom and the man happy, and despite my best efforts, I've been unable to influence their preferences. What can I say? Not everyone is born with a sophisticated palate like mine.

Mom and the man tap their glasses together and share a tender kiss, which makes my fur bristle because I want to be the only recipient of such affection. I should be used to her devoting some quality time to the man by now, but a twinge of jealousy still makes my chest feel tight. I try to ignore it because this is supposed to be a happy occasion, and I'm glad she enjoys his company. While I was skeptical at first, adopting him has worked out better than expected; however, I'm still not in favor of keeping him indefinitely. He and I have reached an understanding, and sometimes I even appreciate his presence, but I'll always be Mom's number one priority.

They're now watching the large TV in the living room and appear to be excited about something. I don't think the TV is alive, and I don't understand why they are so fascinated by it. To be fair, it's emitting consistent feedback that mimics Mom's speech, but there can't possibly be other people hiding behind that thin screen.

I stroll over to Mom and rub against her bare feet, letting her know that I'm in the mood for cuddling. She glances down at me, leans forward, and gently rubs my cheeks, smoothing back my whiskers and letting them spring forward into a perfect fan. I close my eyes and enjoy the caress, softly purring as she scratches behind my ears and massages my neck. I love spending nights at home with her, especially when there's a reason to celebrate. Perhaps it's my birthday, and I've simply forgotten to mark it on my calendar. There can't possibly be another reason for their excitement. I'm hoping for a wonderful surprise tonight and would prefer something delicious and edible.

The dogs are stretched out on the floor, their paws splayed about haphazardly. They certainly occupy a significant amount of space in this residence. While they look peaceful, I've discovered that they become restless when dreaming and are prone to rolling around, flailing their paws, and even occasionally yelping loudly. I find their goofy behavior amusing and try to imagine what they're thinking. They could be chasing each other around the house or recalling an exciting moment from one of their daily outings. I guess we'll never know. They both appear to be oblivious to the fact that today is a special day and a time to celebrate. Given I seem to have forgotten my own birthday, I can't blame them for not remembering it either.

The night progresses happily with another glass of effervescent liquid, several plates of yucky plant food, and an abundance of laughter. Mom gives me plenty of snuggles and back rubs, and I even convince her to throw in an extra handful of treats. I think we should make this our normal routine because it suits me well. Mousey, Ms. Fish, Bow, Ball of Yarn, and the two new cadets on sentry duty all appear to be in high spirits, so I give them the night off to enjoy the festivities.

Without warning, Mom and the man begin to chant in unison with the voice on the TV. They're enthusiastic and have enormous smiles on their faces. I can't help but wonder if it's finally time for them to reveal my birthday present. This is intriguing, and I love that they have gone to such great lengths to make my day so special.

Leslie Popp

When the chanting stops, they throw their hands into the air, cheer, and share a loving embrace. They clap excitedly, and a similar uproar can be heard in nearby residences. The neighborhood becomes quite noisy, which is odd given it's the middle of the night. Generally, all would be quiet, and my subjects would be peacefully nestled in their beds, sleeping soundly. Instead, they're honoring me by applauding and cheering at the height of my prowling hour, when I'm usually one of the few creatures awake. On a normal night, I would be patrolling my territory with Mousey or another scout by my side. I always check on my toys before going to bed to ensure everything is in order, but I don't think anyone will be sleeping tonight.

I approve of this tradition and feel incredibly special, which is saying a lot given that I'm usually the center of attention and universally adored. Even the two dogs are getting into the spirit, wagging their tails and panting loudly. The skittish one hops to her feet and prances around, looking excited but unsure what all the commotion is about. She trots this way and that, and the man ruffles her fur playfully, prompting the limping dog to amble over in search of attention. Watching this touching scene warms my heart, and a part of me is grateful that the man and dogs are in my life. The moment passes, and I remember that I'm supposed to be jealous because they commandeer Mom's attention on a daily basis, which is a distraction I could do without.

A series of loud explosions split the night air, abruptly interrupting the festivities. My fur stands on end, and my ears swivel in the direction of the threatening noises, which vary in volume and cadence. I'm unsure if the source of the alarming sounds is heading toward or away from our current location. With wide eyes and a racing heart, I frantically glance around, trying to pinpoint the booming menace.

Mom and the man seem excited and rush to the window to gaze up at the sky. I catch a glimpse of colorful explosions that light up the dark night. I'm well aware that Mom's hearing is inferior to mine, but she should be concerned about the disruption. I'm puzzled as to why Mom and the man aren't immediately springing into action to prepare for whatever danger is headed this way and emitting the reverberating battle cries.

I trot into the bedroom on shaky legs, hoping the others will follow my lead. I search for a safe place to hide and settle on the confined space under the bed. I lie on my stomach and crawl into the hiding spot, curling up close to the wall. Now we wait to see if the threat breaches our defenses. I've spent countless hours preparing and planning for worst-case scenarios, and I'm hoping that my troops obey their marching orders.

The ear-splitting noises continue with several at a time, followed by silence, and then one or two stray blasts. The unpredictable pattern unnerves me, and I feel like a sitting duck under here. I wish Mom and the man would take cover for their own protection. However, there's barely enough clearance for me under the bed, and Mom will never be able to wriggle into this tight space. Feeling concerned and scared, I take a few slow breaths and try not to think about it. The booms continue, and my anxiety rises as I anticipate something terrible approaching.

Just when I think I can't take it any longer, I hear footsteps approaching and Mom gently calling my name. I can see her feet as she walks around the bed and want to call out for her, but my throat is so dry. I attempt a meow, but it comes out hoarse and faint, and she doesn't hear me. She calls my name again, pacing around the room and checking all the usual spots. Then she drops to her knees and peers under the bed. Our eyes meet, and she gives me a warm smile that instantly calms my nerves. Mom extends her hand and beckons to me, but I'm rooted to the spot and afraid to move. I want to run into her arms, but I also wish she would join me in the safety of this bunker. I always feel more secure in dark, enclosed spaces. She continues to call my name while lying on the floor with both arms extended. I appreciate the effort, but it confirms my earlier suspicion that she would never fit in this protected hideout.

The man enters the room a moment later and positions himself on the floor. He whispers kind words and gives me an encouraging look, showing that he understands the situation and only wants to comfort and aid me in this time of need. Not wanting to be left alone, the dogs soon make an appearance and curl up in the corner of the room. They appear similarly distraught by the thundering sounds, which makes me feel less alone and closer to them than ever before. They are staring at me with wide eyes, and the skittish one is shivering slightly.

The man scoots over and gently pets them while speaking softly. They take comfort in his touch and raise their heads to gaze up at him. Mustering my courage, I crawl out from under the bed and scamper into Mom's outstretched arms. She tenderly embraces me and whispers soothing words. I begin to relax and press myself against her chest, enjoying the warm embrace. She strokes my head, presses her cheek against mine, and kisses my nose. This loving moment shakes me from my fearful stupor, and I feel the tension start to fade. Mom would never let anything harm me. She loves me unconditionally and would use all of her strength and energy to protect me if anything threatened our home. I'm so grateful to have her in my life, and I can't imagine what it would be like if I had chosen another forever home.

We sit like this for a long time, the entire family in one room, waiting out a tense situation and pulling together as a unit. I'm confident we'll get through this if we maintain a united front.

The resounding sounds become less frequent until they eventually cease altogether. No threat ever materializes, and the source of the noise must have moved on to other regions, leaving my kingdom in peace for now.

It will be difficult to sleep after all this excitement, but I never expected to get much rest, and I have the luxury of sleeping in and napping to my heart's content tomorrow. Since my birthday was so rudely interrupted by what I've recently learned are called fireworks, I doubt anyone will blame me.

It's late, and I can't remember the last time Mom was awake at this hour. The man stands up and guides the dogs toward the front door, enticing them with the colorful ropes that they use to lead him up and down the street.

My stomach rumbles, so I wander out to ensure my food is still untouched and exactly how I left it. Everything appears to be in order, with no sign of a disturbance. I begin to chow down happily, crunching loudly on my dry kibble, which is vastly inferior to wet food but will do in a pinch overnight.

I wash it down with a few dainty sips from my water cup, being careful not to splash any on my paws or nose. Food generally lifts my spirits, and today is no exception. I feel rejuvenated and ready to take on the world. After all, I'm another year older and wiser. Who's really keeping track of time? I don't look a day older than when I first adopted Mom, but I'm certainly far more experienced.

The dogs prance into the living room after their neighborhood patrol and resume their usual positions on the couch. They seem relaxed now and sprawl out, turning this way and that until they find a cozy position. Their eyes droop as they drift off to sleep.

Mom and the man perform their nighttime rituals, which involve rubbing water on their faces and using the smelly paste on their teeth. They appear at ease and soon retreat to the bedroom, crawling under the covers to rest.

The house is now completely dark, and the night feels like any other. Attempting to resume my normal activities, I initiate my lockdown procedures. It starts with a stroll around the perimeter of my territory to ensure that all the windows and doors are secure. Then I inspect my food and litter box in case the dogs were curious and caused trouble while my back was turned. Next, I survey my domain, searching for any signs that something is amiss. Everything is quiet, as it should be.

I move on to my favorite part of the night, tucking in my toys and wishing them sweet dreams. Mousey is resting on top of my tower, where we had been playing earlier, and I give him a gentle tap so he knows I'm watching over him as he sleeps. Ms. Fish is lying on the floor nearby, and I sniff her briefly, tickling her with my long whiskers, before doing the same for Bow, Ball of Yarn, and the two new cadets. Everyone is bedded down, so I conclude my safety check and wander off to the bedroom.

"See you in the morning," I whisper over my shoulder. "Get some rest so you'll be ready for playtime tomorrow."

I gracefully leap onto the bed beside Mom and watch her peaceful face as she breathes slowly and evenly. Our lives revolve around each other, and I'm happy to be the center of her world. We need one another, and I realize how much she means to me. I feel safe in her arms and know that she will always love and care for me.

Leaning forward, I nuzzle my forehead against her warm cheek, and she makes a small noise as her eyelids flutter open. She reaches up and pets my back, eliciting a soft purr from deep within my chest. I gingerly step onto her pillow, causing her head to list to one side, and lie down with my chin resting atop her forehead. I purr contentedly as she gently touches my paw and then my nose. I lightly press my paw against Mom's ear and feel her smile. My tail flicks slowly, brushing against her shoulder. After a few minutes, she lies motionless again, and I sigh before closing my eyes and drifting off to sleep. Dreams of breakfast, sunny spots on the floor, playtime with Mousey, and snuggles with Mom dance through my head.

Author's Bio

Leslie Popp is the author of the *Life by Pumpkin* series. Her affinity for writing was ingrained from an early age, starting with elementary school Write-A-Book contests, which she treated as a serious literary pursuit. She works in finance but loves to write about her furry companions, among other subjects. Leslie has always harbored a deep love of animals, and her pets over the years have included hermit crabs, guinea pigs, cats, and dogs. She adheres to the belief that pets are members of the family and deserve respect, love, and their own pillow on the bed. She firmly supports the humane treatment of all animals and is committed to a vegan lifestyle.

Pumpkin's Bio

Pumpkin (2007–2021) was an orange tabby cat with a loving heart and a big personality. He adopted Leslie in 2010 after meeting her at the animal shelter where she volunteered. Pumpkin had been housed there for a year and was overjoyed to find his perfect human and forever home. His curiosity and desire for attention resulted in his many chronicled adventures. Pumpkin did indeed have his own pillow and side of the bed, as well as a dedicated coffee mug for water in case the water in his bowl was not to his liking that day. He brought joy to those around him and is dearly missed.

Leslie Popp

Synopsis

Life by Pumpkin: A Cat's Tale records the wise teachings and endearing adventures of Pumpkin, an orange tabby cat with strong opinions, unbridled self-confidence, and dreams of expanding his territory into distant lands. Pumpkin shares his opinions on using cuteness to influence those around you, the proper punishment for acts of betrayal, and how to handle new four-legged additions to the family. He provides sage advice on how to manage your human, properly train a mouse toy army, defend your territory from intruders, and utilize all available resources to lay crafty plans for world domination. Pumpkin hopes to spread his message far and wide and let the world know that cats, not humans, are actually in charge.

Quotes and Reviews

"As ruler of this realm, I regularly assess my strengths and weaknesses. After years of experience governing my loyal subjects, I have concluded that my greatest strengths are my intelligence, my ability to look adorable, and my skill at making others feel guilty for not doing exactly what I say when I say it. No one should ever disobey my direct commands, but sometimes they need a little nudge to comply."
 - Pumpkin

"This is a wonderful true story about a genius cat with dashing good looks who spends his days mercifully ruling over his extensive territory and loyal subjects. His insight is life-changing, and his teachings should be practiced by all."
- Pumpkin